PUFFIN BOOKS

Editor: Kaye Webb

MORE STORIES TO TELL

Countless teachers and parents, and children too, have had cause to thank Eileen Colwell for her marvellous collections of stories to read at bedtime, on rainy days or days of illness, or at the end of the school day.

Her long experience as a children's librarian and story-teller has taught her to select exactly the sort of stories that suit young readers best, and every one of her earlier collections in Puffins, *Tell Me a Story, Tell Me Another Story, Time for a Story* and *Bad Boys*, is an established favourite in the classroom and home.

But as we all know, the more stories children hear the more they want, so here is another very welcome collection of all sorts of stories by distinguished children's authors such as Joan Aiken, Leila Berg, Margaret Mahy, Paul Biegel, Donald Bisset and Charlotte Hough, and with characters ranging from a fairy cat, a scarecrow, and a family of tortoises to a tanker, a little car, and a cat that swallowed some yeast and swelled to giant size. Certainly there will be plenty here to keep even the most insatiable story-lover happy day after day for as long as the reader will read.

D0496253

MORE STORIES
TO TELL

*

Edited by Eileen Colwell

Illustrated by
Caroline Sharpe

PUFFIN BOOKS

Puffin Books, Penguin Books Ltd, Harmondsworth, Middlesex, England
Penguin Books, 625 Madison Avenue, New York, New York 10022, U.S.A.
Penguin Books Australia Ltd, Ringwood, Victoria, Australia
Penguin Books Canada Ltd, 2801 John Street, Markham, Ontario, Canada L3R 1B4
Penguin Books (N.Z.) Ltd, 182–190 Wairau Road, Auckland 10, New Zealand

—

This collection first published in Puffin Books 1979

—

Made and printed in Great Britain by
Richard Clay (The Chaucer Press), Ltd
Bungay, Suffolk
Set in Monotype Garamond

Contents

6 CONTENTS

Acknowledgements

Grateful acknowledgements are due to the following:

Jonathan Cape Ltd, Doubleday and Company Inc. and Joan Aiken for 'The Baker's Cat' from *A Necklace of Raindrops*, © 1968 by Joan Aiken; B.B.C. Publications and Jean English for 'Tippy Gets Stuck' from *Tippy the Tipper Wagon*; B.B.C. Publications and Margaret Gore for 'Teddy Bear Gets too Fat for his Jacket' from *Little Pig and the Big Potato*; H. E. Todd for 'The Dog Show'; Andre Deutsch and Michael Rosen for 'Who Rolled in the Mud . . .' from *Mind Your Own Business* (1974); Methuen's Children's Books and Ursula Hourihane for 'Rackettypan the Scarecrow' from *Happy-Go-Lucky Stories*; Blackie and Son, Ltd and Leila Berg for 'The Old Woman and the Mouse' from *The Flying Jacket* by Betty Wilshire; Methuen's Children's Books and Elisabeth Roberts for 'A Little Gardening' from *All about Simon and his Grandmother*; Methuen's Children's Books, A M Heath and Co. Ltd, and Donald Bisset for 'The Boy who Growled at Tigers' from *Another Time Stories*; J. M. Dent and Sons Ltd, Helen Hoke Associates and Margaret Mahy for 'A Present from Star' from *The Second Margaret Mahy Story Book*; B.B.C. Publications and John Grant for 'Littlenose the hero' from *Littlenose the Hero*; Vera Colwell for 'The Adventures of Pyp'; J. M. Dent and Sons, Ltd and Paul Biegel for 'The Adventure: The Town Mouse's Story' from *The King of the Copper Mountains*; Abelard-Schuman, Ltd, and Rudolf Neumann for 'The Little Storm' from *The Kind Crocodile* by Rene Rilz; William Heinemann, Ltd and James Reeves for 'The Wind' from *The Wandering Moon*; William Heinemann, Ltd and Charlotte Hough for 'The Magic Pencil' from *Charlotte Hough's Holiday*

Book; Dr Katharine M. Briggs, editor, for 'The Tortoises' Picnic' from *A Dictionary of British Folk Tales, Part A, Volume I*; Faber and Faber, Ltd and Ann Stadon for 'Everything's Horrid Today' from *Pepper Face and Other Stories*; Hodder and Stoughton's Children's Books and Alison Winn for 'If I were a Fish' from *Swings and Things*; B.B.C. Publications and Liane Smith for 'Bertha Gets into Trouble' from *Bertha the Tanker*; Catherine Mason and the Daily Mirror Literary Competition for 'Michael and the Bird'; Chatto and Windus, Ltd and Greenwillow Books, New York, and Richard Hughes for 'The Invitation' from *The Wonder Dog*; Methuen Children's Books and Joseph Capek for 'How Puss and Pup Made a Birthday Cake' from *Harum Scarum*; George G. Harrap and Co., Ltd, and Joan G. Robinson for 'Susie Has some New Shoes' from *Susie at Home*; Sidgwick and Jackson, Ltd and Ffrida Wolfe for 'Choosing Shoes' from *The Very Thing*; Curtis Brown and Pauline Clarke for 'The Cat and the Fiddle' from *Bel the Giant and Other Stories*; Janet Wade for 'Waggertail and the Thief'; The Bodley Head and Margery Clark for 'Erminka and the Red-topped Boots' and 'Erminka and the Duck Pond' from *The Poppy Seed Cakes*, Copyright 1924 by Doubleday and Company Inc. Adapted by permission of Doubleday and Company Inc.

The Baker's Cat

JOAN AIKEN

Once there was an old lady, Mrs Jones, who lived with her cat, Mog. Mrs Jones kept a baker's shop in a little town at the bottom of a valley between two mountains.

Every morning you could see Mrs Jones's light twinkle out, long before all the other houses in the town, because she got up very early to bake loaves and buns and jam tarts and Welsh cakes. First thing in the morning Mrs Jones lit a big fire. Then she made dough out of water and sugar and flour and yeast. Then she put the dough into pans and set it in front of the fire to rise.

Mog got up early too. *He* got up to catch mice. When he had chased all the mice out of the bakery, he wanted to sit in front of the warm fire, but Mrs Jones wouldn't let him, because of the loaves and buns there, rising in their pans.

She said, 'Don't sit on the buns, Mog.'

The buns were rising nicely. They were getting fine and big. That is what yeast does. It makes bread and buns and cakes swell up and get bigger and bigger.

As Mog was not allowed to sit by the fire, he went to play in the sink.

Most cats hate water, but Mog didn't. He loved it. He liked to sit by the tap, hitting the drops of water with his paw as they fell, and getting water all over his whiskers.

What did Mog look like? His back, and his sides, and his legs as far as where his socks would have come to, and his face and ears and his tail were all marmalade coloured. His stomach and his waistcoat and his paws were white. And he had a white tassel at the tip of his tail, white fringes in his ears, and white whiskers. The water made his marmalade fur go almost fox colour and his paws and waistcoat shining-white clean.

But Mrs Jones said, 'Mog, you are getting too excited. You are shaking water all over my pans of buns, just when they are getting nice and big. Run along and play outside.'

Mog was affronted. He put his ears and tail down (when cats are pleased they put their ears and tails *up*) and he went out. It was raining hard.

A rushing, rocky river ran through the middle of the town. Mog went and sat *in* the water and looked for fish. But there were no fish in that part of the river. Mog got wetter and wetter. But he didn't care. Presently he began to sneeze.

Then Mrs Jones opened her door and called, 'Mog! I have put the buns in the oven. You can come in and sit by the fire.'

Mog was so wet that he was shiny all over, as if he had been polished. As he sat by the fire he sneezed nine times.

Mrs Jones said, 'Oh dear, Mog, are you catching a cold?'

She dried him with a towel and gave him some warm milk with yeast in it. (Yeast is good for people when they are poorly.)

Then she left him sitting in front of the fire and began making jam tarts. When she had put the tarts in the oven she went out shopping, taking her umbrella.

But what do you think was happening to Mog?

The yeast was making *him* rise.

As he sat dozing in front of the fire he was growing bigger and bigger.

First he grew as big as a sheep.

Then he grew as big as a donkey.

Then he grew as big as a cart-horse.

Then he grew as big as a hippopotamus.

By now he was too big for Mrs Jones's little kitchen, but he was *far* too big to get through the door. He just burst the walls.

When Mrs Jones came home with her shopping-bag and her umbrella she cried out, 'Mercy me, what is happening to my house?'

The whole house was bulging. It was swaying. Huge whiskers were poking out of the kitchen window. A marma-lade-coloured tail came out of the door. A white paw came out of one bedroom window, and an ear with a white fringe out of the other.

'Morow?' said Mog. He was waking up from his nap and trying to stretch.

Then the whole house fell down.

'Oh Mog!' cried Mrs Jones. '*Look* what you've done.'

The people in the town were very astonished when they saw what had happened. They gave Mrs Jones the Town Hall to live in, because they were so fond of her (and her buns). But they were not so sure about Mog.

The Mayor said, 'Suppose he goes on growing and growing and breaks our Town Hall? Suppose he turns fierce? It would not be safe to have him in the town, he is too big.'

Mrs Jones said, 'Mog is a gentle cat. He would not hurt anybody.'

'We will wait and see about that,' said the Mayor. 'Suppose he sat down on someone? Suppose he was hungry? He had better live outside the town, up on the mountain.'

So everybody shouted, 'Shoo! Scram! Psst! Shoo!' and poor Mog was driven outside the town gates. It was still raining hard. Water was rushing down the mountains. Not that Mog cared.

But poor Mrs Jones was very sad. She began making a new lot of loaves and buns in the Town Hall, crying into them so much that the dough was too wet and very salty.

Mog walked up the valley between the two mountains. By now he was bigger than an elephant – almost as big as a whale! When the sheep on the mountain saw him coming, they were scared to death and galloped away. But he took no notice of them. He was looking for fish in the river. He caught lots of fish! He was having a fine time.

By now it had been raining for so long that Mog heard a

loud watery roar at the top of the valley. He saw a huge wall of water coming towards him. The river was beginning to flood, as more and more rain-water poured down into it off the mountains.

Mog thought, 'If I don't stop that water, all those fine fish will be washed away.'

So he sat down, plump in the middle of the valley, and he spread himself out like a big, fat, cottage-loaf.

The water could not get by.

The people in the town had heard the roar of the flood-water. They were very frightened. The Mayor shouted, 'Run up the mountains before the water gets to the town, or we shall be drowned.'

So they all rushed up the mountains, some on one side of the town, some on the other.

What did they see then?

Why, Mog, sitting in the middle of the valley. Beyond him was a great lake.

'Mrs Jones,' said the Mayor, 'can you make your cat stay till we have built a dam across the valley, to keep all that water back?'

'I will try,' said Mrs Jones. 'He mostly sits still if he is tickled under his chin.'

So for three days everybody in the town took turns tickling Mog under his chin with hay-rakes. He purred and purred and purred. His purring made big waves roll right across the lake of flood-water.

All this time the best builders were making a great dam across the valley.

People brought Mog all sorts of nice things to eat, bowls of cream and condensed milk, liver and bacon, sardines, even chocolate! But he was not very hungry. He had eaten so much fish.

On the third day they finished the dam. The town was safe.

The Mayor said, 'I see now that Mog is a gentle cat. He can live in the Town Hall with you, Mrs Jones. Here is a badge for him to wear.'

The badge was on a silver chain to go round his neck. It said MOG SAVED OUR TOWN.

So Mrs Jones and Mog lived happily ever after in the Town Hall. If you should go to the little town of Carnmog you may see the policeman holding up the traffic while Mog walks through the streets on his way to catch fish in the lake for breakfast. His tail waves above the houses and his whiskers rattle against the upstairs windows. But people know he will not hurt them because he is a gentle cat.

He loves to play in the lake and sometimes he gets so wet that he sneezes. But Mrs Jones is not going to give him any more yeast. He is quite big enough already.

From *A Necklace of Raindrops*

Tippy Gets Stuck

The Story of a Tipper Wagon

JEAN ENGLISH

Tippy, the little tipper wagon, was doing one of the jobs that he really enjoyed. He was driving out to the quarry just outside the town to collect a load of small stones.

A quarry is a place where the stones come from that help to make our roads and paths. It is usually on the side of a hill where all the soil and grass have been dug away till there's lots and lots of stone to be seen, then the men in charge of the quarry dig out all the stone with machines and break it up into little stone chippings. Sometimes they blast the stone out with dynamite, and that can make a very big bang. But Tippy knew that the men are always careful, and warn everybody to get out of the way before they make the big bang, so he was never scared about going to the quarry.

He really enjoyed having his back part filled up with the clean, white, powdery stone chippings. But most of all he enjoyed driving away from the quarry and arriving at the place where the road was being made. Then Bob would pull a lever beside his steering wheel and *whoo-oo-oosh*, down would fall the chippings in a lovely, noisy shower, down on to the roadside.

Already he'd brought two loads of little stones this morning, and he was feeling very happy because he knew he was doing a good job.

'It looks as if we'll be backwards and forwards to the quarry all day, Tippy,' said Bob. 'The workmen will need loads and loads of stones for this road.'

'That's all right, Bob,' said Tippy. 'I like this work.'

'Good lad,' said Bob. 'Here we are, back again at the roadworks. Ready for tipping, Tippy?'

'Ready,' called the little wagon. And *whoo-oo-oosh*, down went the stones with a rush and a crash and a cloud of white powdery dust.

Tippy waited for the bump when Bob would pull the other lever and bring his back part bumping down into its proper position again. But no bump came.

'Come on, Bob, let's be on our way for another load,' called Tippy impatiently.

'Just – just a minute,' said Bob, and he sounded worried. 'I can't seem to move the lever. It's stuck.'

'Stuck?' said Tippy. 'What do you mean?'

Bob didn't answer for a few minutes, he was busy trying

to move the lever. Then he said, 'I'm afraid something's gone wrong with your inside works. I just can't get your back part down again.'

'You mean – you mean I'll have to stay like this, for ever and ever?' asked Tippy.

'Oh no, don't worry, it's not as bad as that,' said Bob. 'But I'm afraid there's no more work for you today. We'll have to go back to the yard and have your insides looked at, so we can find out what's gone wrong.'

'Oh Bob, will I have to go through the streets with my back part sticking up in the air like a sail? I'll feel awfully silly.'

'Never mind. It's not far to the yard. And I'll try to go through only the quietest streets, so not many people will see you,' said Bob, in an understanding way.

So off they set. Tippy did feel funny. He didn't feel ill exactly, but just all funny and wrong. He tried not to notice the little boys on the way who pointed to the bright orange wagon with its tipper back sticking straight up in the air. 'Look at that wagon,' they said to their mothers. 'Oh do look, the driver's forgotten to let the back come down again. Shall we tell him, do you think?'

And their mothers usually said, 'No, no, it really doesn't matter, Andrew,' or Ian, or whatever the little boy's name happened to be. 'Come along, let's get some shopping done.'

At last they reached the yard. Luckily there weren't any of the other wagons to see what a funny sight Tippy looked. But the mechanic was there in the garage, and he couldn't help laughing when he saw Tippy.

'Well, well, well,' he said. 'You are stuck-up today, aren't you?' And he laughed some more. He was a big, red-faced man with a loud voice, and Tippy didn't know him very well.

'Can't – can't *you* see what's the matter with me, Bob?' he asked.

'Oh, I'm only a driver, Tippy, not a mechanic. I wouldn't know how to put you right again,' said Bob. 'Mr Magillicuddy here will know just what to do, once he's had a good look at you.'

'That's right, young man,' boomed Mr Magillicuddy. 'You'll be all right with me. Bob will have to get back on the job.'

'Are you going to drive another wagon, not me?' Tippy asked Bob.

'Just for a little, until you're better,' said Bob. 'I expect the quarry will lend me one for today. Now good-bye, Tippy. Mr Magillicuddy will be just as gentle as he can be, I'm sure. I'll see you tonight.'

'Good-bye, Bob,' said Tippy, and he waited nervously for Mr Magillicuddy to start. He was really just a little bit frightened of the mechanic. He was such a big man, so red-faced, with such a loud voice, and his overalls had black oil stains on them.

'Now, you and me are going to get on famously, Tippy,' he boomed. 'I'm just going to have to poke about in your gearbox a bit, but it'll be all over very soon.'

It did hurt Tippy just the tiniest bit, but it was soon over, and then Mr Magillicuddy said he might as well give Tippy a thorough overhaul.

'Oh dear, what's that?' said Tippy.

'Just a good old clean-up inside, so you'll feel really fit and ready for work tomorrow,' said the mechanic.

And really, Tippy found he quite enjoyed that. It made him feel very well looked after. When Mr Magillicuddy stopped for lunch, and brought out his sandwiches, he gave Tippy a drink of water and sat on a box in the middle of the yard, singing funny songs and telling stories.

By the time Bob came back to the yard that night, the two of them, the little orange wagon and the big red-faced mechanic, were really good friends, and Bob was very pleased to see how Tippy had been behaving himself.

'That's a real fine little wagon you've got there, Bob,' said Mac. 'I've tuned up the engine and he'll go a treat tomorrow, you wait and see.'

And he was quite right. After his day's rest and his thorough overhaul, Tippy worked better than ever next day, and how he enjoyed having his back part tipped up and hearing the stones *whoo-oo-ooshing* down on to the roadway. And he enjoyed even more feeling that lovely *bump* when the back part came safely down once more.

From *Tippy the Tipper Wagon*

Teddy Bear Gets too Fat for his Jacket

MARGARET GORE

One morning when Teddy Bear was doing up his dark blue jacket with the three brass buttons, one of the buttons popped off and fell on the floor. It was the middle button.

'Oh dear,' said Teddy Bear in his deep, growly voice. 'I must be getting fat.'

He looked at himself in the mirror.

'Either I have got fat or the jacket has shrunk. Perhaps it shrank when I got caught in all that rain the other day.'

Then Teddy Bear remembered that he had been wearing his green pullover that day. So it wasn't that.

'There is no doubt about it,' said Teddy Bear. 'I have got too fat and I shall have to do some exercises.'

But by the time Teddy Bear had done arm stretch three times and knees bend twice, he was quite out of breath.

'Oh dear,' he growled. '*That* won't do. I shall have to think of something else. Perhaps my friend Badger who lives on the common can help me.'

So down to the common went Teddy Bear – left, right, left, right, left, right. He found Badger busily digging in the earth.

'Please, Badger, can you help me?' asked Teddy Bear. 'I've got too fat and I can't do up my jacket.'

'You should try digging holes as I do, Teddy Bear,' said Badger, and went on with his digging.

So Teddy Bear took off his jacket with the two buttons on instead of three and began digging. He was tired out after digging up only about one pailful of earth.

'Oh dear,' growled Teddy Bear. '*That* won't do. I don't think bears are meant to dig holes. I'll have to think of something else. Perhaps my friend Brown Dog who lives at the crossroads can help me.'

So off went Teddy Bear again – left, right, left, right, left, right – till he came to the crossroads.

Brown Dog lived in the house on the corner, and there he was, running about in his big garden.

'Please can you help me, Brown Dog?' asked Teddy Bear. 'I've got too fat and I can't do up my jacket.'

'You should do as I do, Teddy Bear,' replied Brown Dog. 'I am always running about – I hardly ever stop except when I go to bed.'

So Teddy Bear ran all the way home without stopping once for a rest, but when he arrived he was so breathless he had to sit down in his armchair and have a few spoonfuls from a tin of sweet milk to make him feel better.

'Oh dear,' growled Teddy Bear. '*That* won't do. I don't think bears are meant to keep on running all the time without stopping. I'll have to think of something else. Perhaps my friend Tabcat will be able to help me.'

Down the road he went again – left, right, left, right, left, right – till he came to Tabcat's home.

He saw Tabcat sitting on top of the high wall that went round his garden.

'Can you help me, Tabcat?' asked Teddy Bear. 'I've got too fat and I can't do up my jacket.'

'You should try jumping, Teddy Bear,' replied Tabcat, looking down at him with his green eyes. 'I am always jumping up on to this wall.'

'Jumping?' said Teddy Bear doubtfully.

Tabcat looked at Teddy Bear's fat little figure standing there and he said kindly: 'Perhaps you could start jumping on to *little* walls first, Teddy Bear. Come with me – I'll show you where there's one.'

Tabcat jumped gracefully down from the high wall and led Teddy Bear into the rose garden.

'There you are, Teddy Bear, there's a nice *low* wall,' said Tabcat. 'Now if you'll excuse me, it's time for my lunch.'

It may have been a low wall to Tabcat, but to Teddy Bear it looked quite high.

However, he went back a few steps, then took a flying leap at the wall. Unfortunately he didn't jump quite high enough and landed on the ground with a hard thud.

'Oooo! Oh dear,' growled Teddy Bear. 'I *certainly* don't think bears were meant to go jumping up on to walls – even if they are low ones.'

He walked sadly home, feeling rather stiff and sore.

On the way back he came to Mrs Duck's shop. Once a week he bought a large jar of honey at Mrs Duck's and to-day was the day for it.

'It's no use,' he said to himself. 'The only way I shall stop being fat is to give up eating sweet things. I must go in and tell Mrs Duck that I shall not be needing any more jars of honey. Oh dear!'

He gave a big sigh, for if there was one thing Teddy Bear did love it was honey. But he bravely pushed open the shop door and went in.

'My goodness, Teddy Bear, you do look tired,' exclaimed Mrs Duck and she made him sit down on a chair.

'I do feel rather weak, Mrs Duck,' replied Teddy Bear. He cast a longing glance at a jar of honey on the shelf.

'Poor Teddy Bear, you probably need something to eat. I'll get you a big cup of cocoa and a chocolate biscuit. Then you'll feel better.'

Teddy Bear held up a weak paw. 'No, no thank you, Mrs Duck, I won't have anything,' he said. 'Not *anything*.'

Mrs Duck stared at Teddy Bear in astonishment. 'You must be ill, Teddy Bear,' she said. 'Perhaps I should call the doctor.'

Then Teddy Bear told her all his troubles and showed her his jacket. 'The middle button came right off this morning,' he said, 'because I am getting fat.'

'Nonsense, Teddy Bear,' laughed Mrs Duck. 'It only means you are growing up into a fine big bear – and who ever heard of a *thin* bear! Now you just stay there, and while you're drinking that cup of cocoa and eating that chocolate biscuit I shall sew on your buttons in a different place. Then you will be able to do up your jacket quite easily, I'm sure. I hope you haven't lost that middle button, Teddy Bear?'

'Oh no, Mrs Duck,' replied Teddy Bear. 'Here it is in my pocket.'

Mrs Duck sewed the buttons on one inch nearer the edge. 'Now, Teddy Bear,' she said, 'Come and try your jacket.'

It was a perfect fit.

'Oh, thank you, Mrs Duck,' cried Teddy Bear. 'Now I must go home – and I'll take a jar of honey with me – a large jar.'

When Teddy Bear arrived home he put the jar of honey on the table and took out a big spoon.

Then he gave a deep, growly laugh.

'Who ever heard of a *thin* bear!' he said.

From *Little Pig and the Big Potato*

The Dog Show

H. E. TODD

Every Wednesday morning at ten o'clock the dogs in the village gathered together on the Green for the weekly meeting of the Lucky Puppy Club. They had been doing this for several years and most of them were no longer puppies, but they still kept the club title because they liked the sound of it.

The President and Founder of the Club was a very serious looking dog with long silky ears and a wise wrinkled face like a judge. His real name was Geoffrey, and everyone called him Judge Geoffrey. Then there were two young puppies, Dibs with a white face and a black spot over his right eye, and Dabs with a white face and a black spot over his left eye. Two very long dogs with one short leg at each corner were called Sausage and Mash. Scamp was a real live wire, which was not surprising because he was a wire-haired terrier. Shaggy was very shaggy indeed and could hardly see through the hair over his eyes. Sally was a fat and lazy spaniel who belonged to Mr and Mrs Butler, but hardly took any notice of them because she was asleep most of the time. And Fifi was a smart poodle who barked with a French accent. She smelt of lavender and her tail and tummy were shaved (except for the fuzzy bit at the end of her tail). She belonged to Lady Fitzherbert.

But on that day one dog was missing – Scruffy. Poor Scruffy! His master, Bill Baxter, did not look after him very well and was not always kind to him, but Scruffy remained

cheerful and no one could dislike him because his tail wagged furiously whatever scatterbrain scrape he was in. He never seemed to remember any order he was given – and had forgotten the meeting that morning. As a matter of fact it was a good thing he had, as otherwise this story would never have been told.

As soon as they arrived, all the dogs could talk about was the Dog Show which was to be part of the Fête being held on the following Saturday in the Vicarage Field.

'Wouldn't it be lovely,' suggested Dibs, 'if *each* of us could win a prize?'

'That's a splendid idea,' said Judge Geoffrey. 'Let's run through the events and work it out.'

Well, the first event was to be the Prettiest Dog so, of course, they all said that Fifi would have no trouble in winning that. Fifi tried to look flattered, but it was easy to see that she expected to win it anyway.

The second event was rather more difficult, because it was for the Longest Dog. It was obvious that either Sausage or Mash would be the winner, but the trouble was that they both looked exactly the same length. Mash said, 'I think I ought to be allowed to win First Prize this time because when Mrs Simmonds entered us for the Long Dog Competition last year, Sausage cheated. He wriggled his nose, so I only got Second Prize.'

'Never mind,' said Judge Geoffrey, 'you're bound to win first and second prize between you. I've an idea how *you* can win this time. Listen!' and he whispered something into Mash's ear and Mash smiled.

After that they went through the list, and it was surprising how easily the prizes could be shared amongst them. Sally would be the fattest dog, Dibs and Dabs the smallest and Shaggy, without doubt, the shaggiest. Scamp would be the cheekiest and Judge Geoffrey the wisest looking.

Then Fifi asked a difficult question. 'What about Scruffy? He never wins a prize, so if he could just once, he would be so pleased that I am sure he would be much more sensible afterwards.'

The trouble was, what could Scruffy possibly win? He wasn't long, he wasn't short, he wasn't pretty, he wasn't very clean, and he didn't smell nice. In any case the only prize left was for the Most Obedient Dog, and Scruffy wasn't at all obedient!

'There's only one way for Scruffy to win,' said Judge Geoffrey. 'During the Competition we shall have to be even more disobedient than he is.'

'Oh dear,' cried Fifi. 'What will Lady Fitzherbert say? She always expects me to win the Most Obedient Dog. I've won it at every Dog Show I've ever entered for. Couldn't I be first and Scruffy second?'

'Certainly not,' said Judge Geoffrey. 'You must join in with our plans or we shall turn you out of the Lucky Puppy Club.'

And that was that.

The following Saturday afternoon was fine and warm and all the people in the village turned up for the Fête. When the time came for the Dog Show, they crowded round a large ring set up in the middle of the field. The man-in-charge was very impressive-looking, with a large bushy moustache.

Fifi easily won the prize for the Prettiest Dog, as expected, and she looked so pleased with herself and paraded so charmingly with Lady Fitzherbert that all the dogs began to worry about the result of the Most Obedient Dog event. When Sausage and Mash entered for the Longest Dog, Sausage again wriggled his nose, but it didn't do him any good this time. Mash took the advice that Judge Geoffrey had whispered to him and stuck his tail out, so he won First Prize and Sausage Second Prize.

Everything went as arranged after that, although the people at the Fête never guessed that the dogs themselves had decided who was to win, not their owners. However, the owners looked very proud of themselves when their dogs won anything, though why Mr Smith, for instance, should be proud of himself because Shaggy happened to be the shaggiest and least brushed dog, is difficult to understand.

At last the time arrived for the Most Obedient Dog Competition. The first dog to be called was Shaggy. Mr Smith led him into the ring but all Shaggy did was to rush round barking at people, he never took any notice of Mr Smith at all. As for Dibs and Dabs, they took no notice of anyone except each other and pretended to fight furiously. Sally went to sleep and although Mrs Butler shouted and shouted at her, she never entered the ring at all, so she could hardly win a prize could she? Neither could Scamp, because he did nothing but pretend to limp about on three legs, although there was nothing whatever wrong with his fourth leg. Sausage and Mash went right to the middle of the ring and started to dig for rats that weren't there, and the more Mr Simmonds asked them to do something else, the deeper they dug till only the tips of their tails could be seen.

Scruffy was called next. Bill Baxter, looking just as scruffy as Scruffy himself, shouted 'Scruffy!' in a rough voice, and Scruffy wandered into the ring. Luckily he did sit down once when his master ordered him to, but it was probably by mistake. Anyway, he did do one thing he was told to do, which was more than any of the other dogs had done.

By that time, all the people were roaring with laughter, and it seemed certain that either Judge Geoffrey or Fifi would win – but what a shock was in store for everyone! Mr Watson called Judge Geoffrey. He ran in, wagging his tail, and then went straight over to the impressive-looking man with the bushy moustache and bit him in the leg! Actually he didn't bite very hard, but the gentleman hopped about making an awful fuss and telling Mr Watson he ought to be ashamed of himself, so that Mr Watson felt like biting his other leg for him.

That left Fifi. Lady Fitzherbert carried her into the ring, looking like a perfect angel. 'Come on, Fifi darling,' she said. 'Show the nice gentleman what a good little doggie you are. Hold up your paw and shake hands with him.'

Fifi turned her back and started scratching herself.

'Don't be silly, Fifi darling,' said Lady Fitzherbert. 'Nice doggies don't scratch.'

Fifi scratched rather harder than before.

Lady Fitzherbert went red in the face. 'I cannot understand it,' she said to the gentleman with the bushy moustache, 'Fifi *never* scratches.'

But Fifi was scratching this time and the more sweetly Lady Fitzherbert begged her not to, the more furiously she scratched. The people laughed, the dogs barked with excitement, but nothing would stop Fifi scratching.

So Scruffy really did win the prize, for after all he *had* obeyed once! He was absolutely delighted and very proud, although he never quite understood why he had been so lucky. Bill Baxter his master was pleased too, and ever since then he and Scruffy have been better friends. What is more, Scruffy has been *much* more sensible, and as a matter of fact, so has Bill Baxter.

Who Rolled in the Mud

MICHAEL ROSEN

Who rolled in the mud
Behind the garage door?
Who left footprints
across the kitchen floor?

I know a dog whose nose is cold
I know a dog whose nose is cold

Who chased raindrops
down the windows?
Who smudged the glass
with the end of his nose?

I know a dog with a cold in his nose
I know a dog with a cold in his nose

Who wants a bath
and a tuppeny ha'penny biscuit?
Who wants to bed down
in his fireside basket?

Me, said Ranzo
I'm the dog with a cold

From *Mind Your Own Business*

Rackettypan the Scarecrow

URSULA HOURIHANE

There was once an old scarecrow who lived in the middle of
a big ploughed field. His name was Rackettypan, and he had
a queer round turnip head with a battered old hat on top to
keep out the rain. Rackettypan wore a long raggedy coat
that had once belonged to Farmer Giles, and he had a
string of shining silvery tin strips hanging from the end of
his thin, stick arms. When the wind blew Whoo-oo!
Rackettypan's tin strips went jingle-jangle, jingle-jangle, and
all the birds that had been scratching out in the ploughed
field for corn to eat flew up into the air with a great crying
and squawking – Caw-Caw! Quee-quee! Caa-caa! they went.
All except the little red-breasted Robin. He didn't mind the
jingle noise at all. He just chirrupped to himself and flew up
on to Rackettypan's old battered hat and sang, 'Sweet,
sweet, sweet!' as hard as he could go. Rackettypan loved
to hear Robin Redbreast singing so gaily.

'That's the way!' he would shout up to him. 'Sing away,
little Robin. Sing away! It does me good to hear you. I get
so lonely in the middle of this big field by myself all day and
all night. Nobody ever stops to talk to me but you.'

And Robin Redbreast would think of all his nicest,
happiest songs to cheer up the lonely old scarecrow.

One day when the long cold winter was nearly over and
the snow that had covered the big ploughed field had begun
to melt, Rackettypan stood shivering as the wind blew
Whoo-oo! right through his torn old coat, and the silvery

tin strips shook and jangled as hard as they could go. There were hardly any birds to frighten off the field, and Racketty-pan hadn't seen his little friend Robin Redbreast for several days. He felt very sad and lonely.

'Brr,' he shivered. 'How cold it is. Won't the warm sunny days ever come?'

And then, suddenly, out of the hedge at the bottom of the field flew Robin Redbreast.

'Hallo!' he called cheerily. 'Shall I tell you something, old scarecrow? The winter is over and the spring is just round the corner. Cheer up! Cheer up! Spring is nearly here.'

Then he flew off again with a great whirr of his wings.

'Well,' said Rackettypan. 'That's good news. Robin always knows. Spring can't be far away and the sunny days will soon be here. How glad I am.'

And, sure enough, before the week was out, the sun came shining through the clouds, the birds began to sing in the hedges, and the buds on the tall trees began to swell fatter and fatter ready to shoot out their fresh young green leaves. Oh, Rackettypan *was* happy!

'I wish Robin would come to see me again,' he said. 'I'd like to tell him how clever he was to guess about spring being so near.' But Robin didn't come all that day. And he didn't come the next day either. Or the next. Or the next. Rackettypan began to get quite anxious.

'I do hope nothing has happened to him,' he said to himself. 'It's not like him to keep away for so long.'

And then, one lovely sunshiny morning when there were fat white clouds blowing gently across the blue sky, Rackettypan heard a quick flutter of wings, felt a gentle little bump on his head, and there was Robin again!

'Sweet, sweet, sweet!' he sang. 'Sweet, sweet, sweet!'

'Oh, there you are at last!' cried Rackettypan gladly. 'Where have you been all this time? I've been quite worried about you.'

'I've a surprise for you,' said Robin Redbreast. 'I've got a wife. Sweet, sweet, sweet!'

'My, my,' said the old scarecrow. 'That is news. Why don't you bring her to see me?'

'She's waiting in the hedge over there,' said Robin, and he flew off to fetch her. What a chattering and chirrupping there was, to be sure.

'Where are you going to live?' Rackettypan asked the Robins at last. 'Don't go too far away, will you? Please come and see me sometimes.'

Robin Redbreast chuckled. 'I should think we would,' he said. 'Do you know where we want to make our nest, Mr Scarecrow? If you will let us, we'd like to live in your big pocket there.'

Oh, Rackettypan was pleased! 'Live in my pocket?' he cried. 'Of course you can! I shall be honoured.'

How hard the little Robins worked. They carried fluff and moss, and twigs and feathers, and bits of horsehair, and they made the snuggest nest you can think of, deep down at the bottom of the old scarecrow's pocket. No matter how cold the winds blew or how hard it rained, the two little Robins were snug and warm, in the shelter of Rackettypan's big pocket. And, at last, one sunshiny day Robin flew up in great excitement to tell Rackettypan that there were five white eggs with red spots on them in the nest. Then, when the hedges were white with hawthorn blossoms and Rackettypan's big field was bright with pale green shoots of young corn, there was a great squeaking and cheeping in the nest, and out hatched five tiny squawking baby Robins. How busy the baby birds kept their father and mother! To and fro they had to fly with mouthfuls of food for their hungry family. There was no time for Robin Redbreast to sit on Rackettypan's head and sing now. But Rackettypan didn't mind. He wasn't lonely any more. He had five noisy chirrupping baby Robins to keep him company.

From *Happy-Go-Lucky Stories*

The Old Woman and the Mouse

LEILA BERG

Once upon a time, an old woman was sweeping her floor, when she found a little hole in it.

'Oho, oho,' she said, chuckling to herself. 'I do believe a little mouse lives down this hole, and at night when I'm asleep, he will pop out and eat my dinner. So,' she said, going down very carefully on her hands and knees, for she was very old and stiff, 'I'll peep down this hole and catch him.'

And she twitched up her skirt and pushed up her sleeves and she put her eye to the hole. There she lay. Head on the floor and tail in the air.

While she was lying there with her eye to the hole, an old man came in.

'Hello, old dear,' he cried. 'What's the matter?'

The old woman moved not a jot. But with her eye to the hole, she said, 'Down this hole lives a little mouse. And at night when I'm asleep, he'll creep out and eat my dinner. So I shall peep down this hole and catch him.'

'And I shall help you, old woman,' cried the man. 'I shall certainly help you.' And he tossed up his coat tails, and hitched up his trousers.

And because there was no room for the two of them to look down the same hole he made a fresh hole in the floor for himself, and stared down that.

And now there were two of them there. Heads on the floor and tails in the air.

While they were watching, the cat came in. 'Ho there, my beauties,' he said. 'What are you doing?'

And without a quiver, with her eye fixed to the hole, the old woman said: 'Down this hole lives a mouse. And in the evening he will certainly pop out and eat up my dinner. So I'm peeping down the hole so I can catch him. And the old man's helping me.'

'Ho!' said the cat. 'That's an excellent idea.' And he swished his tail and flattened his ears. Then with his sharp claws he made a new hole in the floor and lay down beside it.

Now there were three of them there. Heads on the floor and tails in the air.

While they were watching, a duck came in from the yard. 'Alack, alack,' she cried. 'What are you doing there?'

And the little old woman stirred not a ha'pworth, but answered: 'Down this hole is a little mouse. And in the evening when the fire's low, he'll pop out and eat my dinner. So I shall watch down this hole and catch him.'

'And I will too,' cried the duck. And she fluttered her

wings and shook her tail. And she made herself a hole with her strong wide beak, and lay down beside it.

Now there were four. Four lying there. Heads on the floor and tails in the air.

While they were lying there, a fox peeped in. He saw them, all with their eyes stuck fast to the holes, and quiet as quiet he tiptoed to the cupboard.

He took a big loaf, and he swallowed it.

He took a whole fish, and he swallowed it.

He took a meat pie, and he swallowed that too.

He took a round of cheese, and he swallowed that too.

Now there was nothing left in the cupboard. So quiet

as quiet he tiptoed out of the door and closed it behind him.

The little old woman heard the door click fast. And thinking it was someone else who might look with them, she cried out: 'A little mouse lives down this hole. And at night when I'm sleepy, he'll creep out and run to my cupboard. So I'm watching by this hole, and I'll catch him.'

And all the others called out: 'Make your own hole beside us.'

'I have made my own hole,' cried the fox from the other side of the door. 'And I've made it in your cupboard. And I've eaten up everything I could find there, so there's nothing left for the poor little mouse.'

Up jumped the little old woman, the little old man, the cat and the duck. But by the time they had the door open, the fox was away over the wall, and over the hill, and all they could see of him was a cloud of dust.

So the little old woman had nothing for dinner at all.

From *The Flying Jacket*

A Little Gardening

ELISABETH ROBERTS

'I was thinking of doing a little gardening,' said Grandmother one afternoon.

'Oh,' said Simon. 'I think I'm going to be very busy doing some sticking in.'

'I must look for the key to the garden shed,' Grandmother said thoughtfully. 'I expect some of the tools need oiling.'

Simon looked interested. 'Have you got a squirting oil-can?' he inquired.

'Of course,' Grandmother said, 'a big one.'

Simon put down the pot of glue he was holding.

'I think I'd better come and help you,' he said. 'I expect some of your tools will be quite heavy to move.'

So Grandmother found the key to the toolshed and they both went downstairs, and down the steps into the garden. This was divided into two halves. One piece belonged to the ground-floor flat and the other half, with the toolshed, belonged to Grandmother. She had a small lawn and two rose-beds, with a narrow stony path which ran round everything. Also, between the garden and the road way, there was a dense green hedge which always needed cutting.

'Gracious me!' Grandmother exclaimed, as she looked at it. 'This hedge is covered in whiskers again! It's only a little while since I cut it.'

'The grass is very sprouty-looking too,' said Simon. 'You could have a hayfield if you left it.'

The key grated stiffly in the lock as Grandmother opened the garden shed.

'Oh dear,' she said ruefully, looking in, 'everything seems to be in rather a muddle.'

Simon squeezed between the lawnmower and an ancient deckchair and went inside. He sniffed loudly. 'There's a very interesting smell in here,' he said.

'You're right,' said Grandmother, 'there is.' She grasped the handle of the lawnmower. 'There's only one thing to do,' she said firmly. 'We must pull everything out and let some fresh air in.'

Simon held on to the deckchair as Grandmother rattled the lawnmower out on the path.

'That sounds very clanky,' he said with satisfaction. 'It's going to need a lot of oiling.'

Then they both started to empty the shed. There were a great many garden tools. There was also an ancient bicycle which was taking up a lot of room at the back, and finally Grandmother hauled out a greasy red can with a long spout.

'There's the oil-can,' she said. 'I think it's got some oil in it.'

Simon pressed the little lever down hard on the top of the can. A thick stream of greeny-yellow liquid spurted suddenly out of the end of it. He wiped his shoe on the grass.

'Yes,' he said, 'it has quite a lot.'

'I shouldn't waste it,' Grandmother said mildly. She picked up a pair of garden shears, and opened and closed them stiffly, several times. 'You'd better begin with these,' she said, 'then I can make a start on the hedge.'

Simon gave the centre of the shears a hearty squirt.

'Whoops!' said Grandmother, stepping back. 'Just a few drops will do.' She tried the shears again and nodded. 'Splendid!' she said. 'I'll set to work at once.' She turned round and advanced towards the hedge clicking the shears fiercely at it.

'Whoops!' said Simon, 'now I'll do the lawnmower.' He squirted oil into all the little holes he could find and tried pushing the mower to and fro several times. 'You still sound rather clanky,' he said to it. 'I'd better wait till the oil goes in a bit.'

After that he decided to begin on the old bicycle. He oiled the wheels and the spokes. Then he did the pedals and the chain. He put a few drops of oil under the saddle, and on the place where the handlebars twisted in the middle.

'It's lucky the bell hasn't got a top on it,' he said, looking at it, 'I can give it a nice little oiling right inside.'

By the time he had finished, Grandmother had neatly clipped the whole of one side of the hedge. She came across the lawn.

'I'm about to sit down for a few moments,' she announced. 'How are you getting on?'

'Could you do the sitting on your bicycle?' asked Simon. 'I've been getting it ready for you.'

Grandmother looked at it doubtfully. She chuckled suddenly and put down the shears.

'I'll have a try,' she said. 'I wonder if it still fits me?'

Carefully she put a foot on one pedal and hoisted herself on to the saddle. Then off she went, wobbling along the path beside the lawn and round the two rose-beds, until she was approaching Simon again.

'Help!' she gasped. She pedalled swiftly past him. 'The brakes aren't working. How am I going to stop?'

She was on her way round the garden for the second time when Simon ran after her.

'Get ready to jump,' he called. 'I'm going to grab you!'

He raced to the front of the bicycle, and catching hold of one side of the handlebars, he held on with all his might.

'Leap for your life,' cried Grandmother. The bicycle stopped so suddenly that she lost her balance and they all tumbled sideways on the grass.

Grandmother gazed at the sky for a moment.

'I'm glad it wasn't the rose-bed,' she said dreamily. Then she sat up slowly and looked at herself. 'You've certainly oiled the bicycle very well,' she remarked. She wiped a smear off her arm.

But Simon was watching the back wheel which was still spinning round gently all by itself. His face wore a pleased look.

'It isn't squeaking at all,' he said.

Grandmother got up stiffly from the grass.

'Oh dear,' she said, 'I think I am. I shall go and have a sit in the deckchair.'

Not long afterwards Prue and her mother emerged from the front door of the downstairs flat. Simon came out of the toolshed and went to show Prue the oil-can. Further down the garden, Grandmother was stretched out on the deck-chair with her eyes shut.

'We're doing a little gardening,' Simon said.

'Very nice,' said Prue's mother. 'We're just going shop-ping.'

Simon gave the oil-can two big squirts to show Prue how it worked.

'I could stay here and help you,' she said at once.

'Oh no, you couldn't,' said her mother firmly. She looked at the oil on Simon's trousers. 'I shall need you to help me to carry things.'

'I don't expect we shall be long,' Prue said hopefully. She followed her mother through the small iron gate and left it to clang noisily after her.

'I'd quite forgotten about that gate,' said Simon when they had gone. He examined its rusty hinges and lifted the oil-can. 'This will want a lot of extra oil, because people are going in and out of it all the time,' he said.

When he'd finished squirting all the rusty bits of the gate, there was still some oil left in the can. Simon looked down the front of himself.

'I expect I shall be needing to have a little wash soon,' he said thoughtfully. He saw that Grandmother still seemed to be very comfortable in her deckchair. Then he gave the oil-can a little shake and started walking towards the house. 'But it would be a pity not to use this all up first,' he decided. He ran up the steps and disappeared inside.

When he came out again, Grandmother was busy putting the tools back in the garden shed.

'I've a feeling it's time for tea,' she said firmly. 'I shall finish the hedge tomorrow.'

'Here's the oil-can,' said Simon. He handed it in. 'It's empty.'

'How surprising,' said Grandmother. She shut the shed door and locked it. This time the key swung easily, and a little oil trickled out of the keyhole.

'That's better,' Grandmother held the key carefully in two fingers. 'I see you've been busy.'

'I have.' Simon was on his way towards the house. 'But wait till you see the kitchen,' he said. 'I've oiled *everything* for you.'

'My goodness,' said Grandmother, 'have you?' She began to hurry after him.

'My goodness, I have,' said Simon, 'and it took ages and ages.'

They couldn't have tea till Grandmother had found a big cloth and done a lot of wiping up.

'It wasn't so drippy when I left it,' Simon looked at the trickle of oil running down the door.

'That's why you need only a little,' said Grandmother, wiping the cold tap before she filled the kettle. She also wiped the light switches and the drawer handles, and then she rubbed the chair seats before they sat down. 'Oil takes you by surprise,' she said.

Simon smiled suddenly. 'I forgot to tell you,' he said. 'I've oiled the front gate all over. I expect Prue and her mother will be taken by surprise when they get home.'

'What!' exclaimed Grandmother.

'I *like* gardening,' said Simon. 'I'll help you again to-morrow.'

From *All About Simon and his Grandmother*

The Apple Tree

If I were an apple
And grew upon a tree,
I think I'd fall down
On a good boy like me.
I wouldn't stay there
Giving nobody joy,
I'd fall down at once
And say 'Eat me, my boy!'

ANON

The Dog and the Bear

TRADITIONAL

This is a story which is told to children in Russia. There are several different versions of it, but I like this one best. It is the story of two friends, a dog and a bear. Here it is.

Long ago in Russia, there was a dog who lived on a farm. He was a big dog with a rough coat and he was so fierce and growled so loudly that bad men who tried to steal a fat hen or a piglet dare not come any nearer. Because he was such a good watch dog, his master fed him well and often gave him a juicy bone to chew.

In time the dog grew old. His teeth were not as sharp and his growl was not as frightening as it used to be. Sometimes he fell asleep when he was on guard and didn't even know thieves were approaching.

One day a fox killed several hens but the dog heard nothing, for he had grown a little deaf. His master was very angry. 'What use are you!' he scolded. 'I shall buy a young dog in your place. Be off with you and find your own food – you'll get no more from me.'

The poor dog was sad to leave his home like this. He had no idea where he could go, so he wandered off into the forest, his tail between his legs. He followed the track of some field mice and a hare or two, but he caught nothing and day by day he grew hungrier and weaker.

One day as he was crouching under some bushes, feeling very sorry for himself, a big brown bear came along. He caught sight of the dog, sniffed him and found him harmless and said, 'What is the matter, dog?'

'My master has turned me out because I am old,' said the dog. 'I have been trying to find some food, for I am very hungry. My master kept me tied up and fed me for so long that I have never learned to hunt for myself.'

'There is plenty to eat in the forest if you know where to look for it,' said the bear. 'What about some honey – or a mouthful of berries?'

'I don't think I should like honey, it's so sticky. And seeds and berries are for birds, not dogs.'

'Bears like them too and honey is delicious,' said the bear, licking his lips at the thought. 'However, everyone to his taste. Let's try hunting together. Perhaps it will be easier for both of us that way. I am getting old too and I can no longer smell as well as I used to.'

So the two animals hunted together and shared all they caught. The dog picked up the scent more quickly than the bear, but the bear was quicker at the kill. Sometimes the bear caught fish for them both. But when the bear dug up anthills, the dog kept away for the ants bit him and tickled his nose.

But hunting was hard work so one day the dog said, 'Supposing we go to my master's house and look round. My master has a baby who lies in a cradle outside the kitchen door when the sun shines. You seize the child and run off with it – I'll chase you and you pretend to be very fierce. Then you must drop the child and I will guard it until my master comes. He will be so pleased that I have saved the baby's life that he will feed me again perhaps. If he does, I shall be sure to find something for you.'

The bear agreed. So on the next sunny day the friends hid and watched the farm. Presently the baby was brought out in his cradle and left in the sunshine.

The huge bear shambled across the farmyard and picked up the child by his clothes. But the old dog chased the bear, making as much noise as he could, barking and snapping and growling. The bear dropped the child but the dog stayed by its side. When the farmer arrived, the child was howling with fright but unharmed. The new dog never appeared at all – he was too frightened of the great bear.

'Well done, old friend,' said the farmer, patting the dog's head. 'You are a better guard than the new dog. Come home with me and I will feed you as long as you keep watch over my son.'

The dog trotted off with the farmer. Now he was fed each

day. All he had to do was sit by the baby and bark fiercely now and then to show he was awake. Each evening the bear came to the back of the farmhouse and the dog gave him some titbit or told him where he could find a tasty meal.

Time passed and one day the farmer's eldest daughter was to be married. The neighbours for miles around were invited to the wedding feast.

'Let me come into the house,' the bear asked the dog. 'I like music and sweet cakes.'

'How can I let you in,' protested the dog. 'Someone will see you and I shall get into trouble and be turned out again.'

'No one will notice me among so many guests,' said the bear. 'I'll stay in a dark corner all the time.'

All went well at first. The bear slipped into the house when there was plenty of noise and the guests were drinking the health of the bride. He sat hunched up in a dark corner and no one noticed him. In fact several people passed him cakes and sweet tea over their shoulders, for they thought he was a shy guest who didn't like to ask for the good things.

Then as the drink flowed and the guests became more and more excited, there were calls for the fiddler to play for dancing. He struck up a gay tune and the guests stamped and clapped their hands to the music as Russians do.

The bear liked the music too and began to stamp. But there wasn't room in the dark corner so he came out into the middle of the room and joined the dancers. There he stood swaying in time to the music and singing – or rather growling – a bear's song as loudly as he could. He felt very happy.

'Just look, it's a bear!' shouted a child in terror. The guests began to scream and run about wildly and the bear, who was not used to so much noise, was confused. His only thought was to get away to the forest, but before he could escape, the men beat him cruelly. The dog could do nothing to help his friend, but at last the bear reached the safety of the forest and the men gave up the chase.

The bear did not dare to come near the farm again and the old dog missed him. He was bored too, with minding the baby who pulled his tail and tweaked his ears most painfully. So one day the dog walked away into the forest and joined his friend again. In time the dog and the bear grew to be quite clever hunters and seldom went hungry. As far as I know, they are still living happily together in the forest.

Advice

Don't sit on an ant-hill,
Whatever you do;
The ants won't like it
And neither will you.

ANON

The Boy who Growled at Tigers

DONALD BISSET

Once upon a time there was a little Indian boy whose name was Sudi, who growled at tigers.

'You be careful,' his mother told him. 'Tigers don't like being growled at.'

But Sudi didn't care and, one day, when his mother was out shopping, he went for a walk to find a tiger to growl at.

He hadn't gone very far when he saw one hiding behind a tree waiting for him to come along so that he could chase him.

As soon as Sudi came up the tiger sprang out and growled, 'GRRRRRGRRRRRRRGRRRRRGRRRRRRR.' And Sudi growled right back, 'GRRRRGRRRRRRGRRRRRGRRRRR-RRRR.'

The tiger *was* annoyed!

'What does he think I am?' he thought. 'A squirrel? A rabbit? A ocelot? ER . . . An ocelot?'

So, next day, when he saw Sudi coming, he sprang out from behind the tree and growled louder than ever 'GRRRRGRRRRRGRRRRRGRRRRRGRRRRR!!!!!!'

'Nice tiger!' said Sudi, and stroked him.

The tiger couldn't bear it and went away and sharpened his claws and lashed his tail and practised growling.

'I am a tiger!' he said. 'T-I-G-E-R; TIGER, GRRR!' When he had finished he looked at his reflection in the water. There was a lovely yellow tiger with black stripes and a long tail. He growled again so loudly that he frightened even himself, and ran away. At last he stopped.

'What am I running away for?' he thought. 'It's only me. Oh dear, that boy has upset me! I wonder why he growls at tigers?'

Next day, when Sudi passed, he stopped him.

'Why do you growl at tigers?' he said.

'Well,' said Sudi, 'it's because I'm shy really. And if I growl at tigers it sort of makes up for it, if you see what I mean.'

'I see!' said the tiger.

'After all,' said Sudi, 'tigers are the fiercest animals in the world and it's very brave to growl at them.'

The tiger *was* pleased.

'Fiercer than lions?' he said.

'Oh yes!' said Sudi.

'And bears?'

'Much fiercer.'

The tiger purred and felt very friendly.

'You *are* a nice boy!' he said and gave him a lick.

After that they often went for walks together and growled at each other.

From *Another Time Stories*

A Present from Star

MARGARET MAHY

When winter came there were frosty mornings and the cold began to nip Penny's knees.

'My feet are warm in their socks and the rest of me is warm too,' she said, 'but my knees are in between, and the cold gets them, Mummy.'

'Well,' said Mummy, 'we'll have to do something about that,' and she did not forget. She bought Penny a pair of green tights. They looked like long green stockings when Penny wore them and felt very warm and comfy indeed. Penny liked putting them on every morning.

'No more cold knees now I've got these green grasshopper legs,' she said. 'I love wearing these tights, Mummy.'

'Well,' said Mummy, 'they look very cosy, but you're getting them a bit dirty. They'll have to be washed to-morrow if it's fine.'

The next day was fine and sunny.

'Your tights will be dry in no time,' said Mummy as she pegged them out. They looked like funny green legs kicking on the line in the winter wind.

Penny and her mother went in to make lunch. Penny watched the toast and did not burn a single piece. After lunch the sun went in behind the clouds and it began to get really cold again.

'Mummy, can I go to the line and see if my tights are dry?' Penny asked.

'Well,' said Mummy, 'I don't expect they will be yet, but you never know with a good wind . . . go and see if you like.'

Off ran Penny down the path to the clothes-line. She looked for her tights and stared in amazement. There they were, dangling on the line, but they didn't look like tights any more, they didn't look like anything except rags. The feet were gone, the knees were gone. Penny could not understand it. What could have happened to her tights? Then an unexpected voice said:

'Mehhhhh!'

Penny jumped in fright and turned round. There, under the spindleberry tree, was a white animal with horns and a beard. It blinked yellow eyes at her and said, 'Mehhh!' It was Mrs Simon's goat, Star.

Penny had often seen Star over Mrs Simon's fence eating the grassy bits of Mrs Simon's garden.

She was suddenly scared of those yellow eyes and curling horns. She ran back up the path calling, 'Mummy, Mummy!' as loudly as she could.

As she came up the path she was pleased to see Mrs Simon herself standing on the step with a collar and chain in her hand.

Penny guessed she was looking for Star.

'Star's here!' she called. 'Star's here, eating my tights.'

Mrs Simon and Mummy ran down the path, and Penny ran close behind them. Star was nibbling the bushes. She stopped and looked at them. Her horns looked curlier than ever.

'That's my naughty Star,' said Mrs Simon. She held out an apple and Star came daintily over to get it.

'Won't she horn us?' Penny asked nervously.

'No, she's very tame,' said Mrs Simon. 'But she is greedy too. She must have liked the green look of your tights.'

'She's even eaten the knees!' said Penny.

'Never mind!' said Mummy. 'It's been an adventure for us, hasn't it. It isn't every day we have a goat visitor. Can you tie her up to the garage door perhaps, Mrs Simon, and come in and have a cup of tea?'

'Santa Claus has a beard like Star's,' Penny said as Mrs Simon put a collar round Star's neck, 'but no horns.'

'He doesn't eat the washing either,' said Mrs Simon.

The next day, when Penny came home from play centre, there was a parcel waiting for her. She opened it, very excited, and found inside *two* pairs of tights, a green pair and a red pair. There was a card with them that said, 'A present to Penny.' Then at the bottom it said, 'Those other tights were most delicious! With love from Goat Star.'

From *The Second Margaret Mahy Story Book*

Littlenose the Hero

JOHN GRANT

It was a wet afternoon, and Littlenose was bored. He was also in disgrace. Father wagged a finger at him and exclaimed: 'That's the last time you come hunting with me. To think of it! In front of all those men! I'm surprised they still speak to me. You ought to hang your head in shame.'

But Littlenose didn't. He wasn't even listening particularly. He was used to this sort of thing.

'When I was your age,' went on Father, 'I was the sole support of my old mother. I was an expert hunter, and my spear-throwing was the talk of the whole tribe.'

Actually, Littlenose's was too; but only because when Father had tried to teach him he had succeeded in hurling a spear through a neighbour's best furs which had been hung out to dry.

Father really was a first-class hunter. What's more, he wanted Littlenose to be one when he grew up. Now, there were no schools in those days, and a boy had to rely on his parents for everything he needed to learn. Sometimes this was very boring, but sometimes it could be more exciting than any school. Father had already taken Littlenose on hunting trips, but this last one had been different. Littlenose had been allowed to help instead of just looking on.

'There must be something you can get right,' continued Father despairingly. 'When we let you do the tracking you led us right into a lions' den; and we only got away because the camp fire we asked you to light set the forest

ablaze and we managed to escape in the smoke. I just don't know!' And he gazed sadly into the fire.

Poor Littlenose! He really did try hard. He really did want to grow up to be as good a hunter as Father. He had a wonderful day-dream in which Father was surrounded by wild animals, including at least three woolly rhinoceros, and only he, Littlenose, could save him; which he did with great dash and bravery and so became the hero of the tribe. But he knew that it would more likely end with his being chased up a tree or eaten by something.

Littlenose went to bed that night very downcast, and over breakfast next morning he sat silently and thought and thought. There must be some way he could show Father that he wasn't as stupid as everyone imagined. He was still thinking as he went out to play with Two-Eyes, his pet mammoth. He didn't even notice one man call jokingly to his wife, 'Watch the washing! Here comes the spear champion!' or another who was trying to light a fire and cried, 'Come and help, Littlenose! You can light bigger fires than any of us!'

Littlenose spent most of the morning sitting under his favourite tree with Two-Eyes and eventually thought of a plan. He must hunt something . . . all by himself. What to hunt and how, was the problem. Small game, birds and rabbits were killed with sticks and stones. But Littlenose's stick and stone throwing was at the best of times unreliable. Horses and deer were either stalked and speared, or chased and stampeded over a big rock. But Littlenose's stalking was most likely to *cause* a stampede, and as for chasing, the animals usually got the wrong idea and chased Littlenose instead!

'If I want to be a great hunter, I must hunt something really big,' he thought. 'Like a rhinoceros.'

He had heard his father speak of how some tribes had caught these huge bad-tempered creatures. First, they dug a large hole in the ground. Then they covered the hole with tree branches and leaves and grass, until no one would ever suspect that the gound wasn't solid, and neither would the rhinoceros. When one came along, the branches broke under its weight, and it fell into the hole. It was beautifully simple. What happened next, like getting the rhinoceros out of the hole and taking it home, was something that Little-nose didn't even consider.

First thing after lunch he started digging. He had a spade made from the flat bone tied to a stick, and found it much harder work than he had imagined. There were rocks to be moved, and tree roots to be chopped through. His arms and shoulders ached, but by supper-time he had something to show for his effort. The hole was at least knee-deep. Carefully, he hid his spade in some bushes and went home.

Mother was appalled when she saw him. 'What have you been doing?' she exclaimed.

'Just playing,' said Littlenose. 'Is supper ready?'

'There's no supper for you, young man, until you scrub all that dirt off, *and* change your furs. You're absolutely filthy. I just don't know how you do it!'

At bedtime it was the same. Littlenose came home even dirtier.

In the days that followed, Mother became very worried about Littlenose. He was out of bed every morning as soon as it was light, instead of having to be dragged out. Except for meal times, he was out of the cave all day, instead of having to be chased out every few minutes by Mother while she tried to get on with the housework. Except for his getting so dirty, he was like a new boy!

Meanwhile the hole was getting bigger. Knee-deep, then waist-deep, then shoulder-deep. Soon, Littlenose couldn't see out as he dug, but he kept on. A rhinoceros was a very big creature and the trap must be large enough. Littlenose was worried in case someone should find out what he was doing. He wanted it to be a surprise when he arrived home with his rhinoceros.

At last the hole was finished. Now came the next part of the work. Littlenose searched the woods round about, and collected all the fallen branches he could see. With Two-Eyes' help, he laid them across the hole in all directions until it was completely covered. Then he spread dead leaves and grass over the branches, and sprinkled earth over that, until you would never have guessed that a deep pit lay underneath.

All he needed now was a rhinoceros.

Looking at the sun, Littlenose realized that it was getting late. It was long past suppertime. He had better hurry. He gave a last sprinkling of grass to his rhinoceros trap, and ran with Two-Eyes towards home.

Mother was furious when he reached the cave. 'Littlenose,' she shrieked, 'you get more exasperating every day. Where have you been? Father's gone to look for you. You'd better run after him and call him back or he'll be out all night.'

Littlenose ran out of the cave to look for Father. He went along by the river, up on the hill, into the woods. But there was no sign of him. He decided that Father must have gone home, and that he had better do likewise or he would be in trouble.

He had only taken a few steps, however, when he heard a dreadful commotion. It sounded like a very large and very angry animal. He looked quickly for a handy tree to climb, then stopped. He listened again . . . and his heart leaped!

His trap! It had worked! He had caught something!

Littlenose ran as quickly as he could. The noises coming from the hole when he reached it were blood-curdling. He dropped on to all fours and crept carefully forward. The shadows in the pit made it difficult to see much, but as his eyes grew accustomed to the dim light, he saw, covered with earth, dead leaves and grass, and roaring with rage as he tried to climb out . . . Father!

For a dreadful moment there was silence. Then Father bellowed, 'Don't just stand there! Get me out!'

Littlenose looked around. He saw a slender sapling growing by the pit. 'Don't go away, Father. I'll be back,' he said, and dashed for home.

Mother was startled when Littlenose rushed into the cave, seized an axe and rushed out again. Back at the trap, he quickly chopped through the stem of the sapling, so that it toppled over with one end in the hole. In a moment Father had scrambled up and out.

Littlenose had just decided to run when, to his astonishment, there was a great burst of cheering.

All the men of the tribe were gathered round and he was lifted up on to broad shoulders and carried at the head of a torchlight procession. Littlenose was set down before the Old Man, the leader of the tribe. He made a long speech, most of which Littlenose didn't understand. He could see Father with a very odd expression on his face, and Mother smiling as the Old Man said . . . 'and so, to a brave boy who saved his father from the perils of the dark forest, I present this token.' And he handed Littlenose a boy-sized spear.

And so Littlenose became a hero, not that it made any real difference. He was still the naughty boy of the tribe and even if he had rescued Father from the rhinoceros trap, Father had a pretty good idea whose fault it was that he had required rescuing in the first place. In almost no time at all Littlenose and Two-Eyes were playing happily together with no thoughts of brave deeds, but simply having fun.

From *Littlenose the Hero*

Quite So

Come into the Ark, said Noah to the animals,
Come into the Ark, my pets;
In walked the elephants, the frogs and the horses,
The cows and the cats and the little marmosets.

Come, said Noah, to the birds and the insects,
Come into the Ark, my loves;
In went the larks and the bees and the beetles,
The butterflies, the robins, the earwigs and the doves.

Come into the Ark, said Noah to the fishes,
Come into the Ark with me –
No, said the shrimps and the whales and the herrings –
There's far more room in the sea!

ANON

Judy and the Fairy Cat

A story from Ireland

Late one Hallowe'en an old woman called Judy was sitting up spinning.

There came a soft knock at the door.

'Who's there?' she asked.

There was no answer, but another knock.

'Who's there?' she asked a second time.

Still no answer, but a third knock. At that the old woman got up in anger.

'Who's there?' she cried again.

A small voice, like a child's, sobbed: 'Ah, Judy dear, let me in! I am so cold and hungry! Open the door, Judy dear, and let me sit by the fire and dry myself! Judy, dear, let me in! Oh-let-me-in!'

Judy, thinking that it must be a small child who had lost his way, ran to the door and opened it. In walked a large black cat waving her tail, and two black kittens followed

her. They walked deliberately across the floor, and sat down before the fire, and began to warm themselves and lick their fur, purring all the time. Judy never said a word, but closed the door and went back to her spinning.

At last the black cat spoke.

'Judy dear,' she said, 'do not sit up so late. This is the Fairies' holiday and they wish to hold a meeting in your kitchen, and eat their supper here. They are very angry because you are still up, and they cannot come in. I and my two kittens have protected you from them. So take my advice and do not interfere with the Fairies' Hallowe'en. But give me some milk, for I must be off.'

Well, Judy got up in a great fright and ran as fast as she could, and brought three saucers full of milk, and set them on the floor before the cats. They lapped up all the milk, then the black cat called her daughters and stood up.

'Thank you, Judy dear,' she said. 'You have been very kind to me, and I'll not forget. Good night! Good night!'

And with that she and her kittens whisked up the chimney and were gone.

Then Judy saw something shining on the hearth. She picked it up; it was a piece of silver money, more than she could earn in a month. She put out the light, and went to bed; and never again did she sit up late on Hallowe'en and interfere with Fairy hours.

The Adventures of Pyp

VERA COLWELL

'There goes Pyp!' cried the children, for everyone knew the little green car. His paintwork and windows shone and he hummed as he sped along the country roads, with Miss Peters to guide him. He liked the sunny days best but sometimes he had to go out on winter days too.

One day when the snow was on the ground, Pyp set out to take Miss Peters to school. Bump! Bump! They went over the hard snow in the lanes, until they came to the little village school. The children were in the playground muffled up in their coats and red and yellow scarves. 'Here comes Pyp!' they shouted.

The little green car swung in at the open gates. The children ran to help Miss Peters cover him up with a large blue rug and the bell rang for school.

After dinner the boys and girls came out to play in the snow. The boys threw snowballs and so did the girls. 'Don't hit Pyp,' called Jane as the snowballs flew through the air, but Pyp, snug and warm under his rug, liked to listen to their laughter and fun.

Lessons ended early because of the snow and at three o'clock the children came tumbling out of the school door. The snow was falling fast and a cold wind blew it about. 'Here comes Miss Peters,' said the children and they helped her to fold up Pyp's rug.

'Jump in,' said Miss Peters opening Pyp's door. 'Three of you in the back and John can sit in the front with me.'

PURR-RR went Pyp's engine, PURR-RR, then stopped. 'Poor Pyp's cold,' said Pauline. PURR-RR-RR said Pyp again – and he was off. 'Good-bye!' shouted the other children as the little car moved carefully through the gates.

'Shall we get home safely?' whispered little Anne anxiously.

'Of course we shall, silly,' said Jane.

'Sit still and Pyp will take you home quite safely,' Miss Peters said.

The fields were white with snow, the trees looked black against it and the snowflakes still came down. Some sheep stood against a wall. 'Baa-a, ba-a-a,' they cried. Cows were making their way to the farm, glad to go into the warm barns to be milked.

PURR-PURR-PURR went Pyp along the snowy road, but soon his hum turned to PURR-RR as he tried to climb up a hill. 'Oh dear!' said Miss Peters. Pyp was stuck!

'Come on, Pyp!' shouted David. 'Try hard – you can do it!'

PURR, PURR-RR-RR! gasped Pyp, but it was no good. His wheels whizzed round and round in the snow without moving an inch.

'No good – you'll have to get out, children,' said Miss Peters sadly.

'We'll push!' said the children, tumbling out of the car.

A large lorry came slowly out of the farm gate. 'Hello!' called the driver. 'You seem in trouble. Can I help you?'

'Oh, please do!' begged Miss Peters.

Down jumped the driver and put his whole weight behind Pyp. 'Now – REV UP!' he shouted and pushed with all his might.

PURR-RRR-RRR-SWISH – with a sudden jerk, Pyp was off.

'Wait for us,' called the children, running up the hill. 'Pyp, Pyp!'

They clambered into the car. 'Phew!' said David. 'I thought we should have to walk home.'

Pyp hurried on. The sky grew darker and the wind blew more keenly. Pyp's lights went on and shone across the snow.

Anne pressed her nose against the window. 'I can just see some houses,' she said. 'We're nearly home.'

And so they were. Lighted windows shed a warm brightness over the road. TOOT-TOOT called Pyp and doors opened and mothers came running out to welcome the children.

Out they all jumped. 'Good-bye, Miss Peters. Thank you for bringing us,' they shouted and Pyp and Miss Peters set off again along the road.

Soon Pyp was shut up in his own little garage. How glad he was to be there. TOOT-TOOT, said the little green car sleepily. TOO-OOO---OO.

Pyp was asleep.

The Adventure: The Town Mouse's Story

PAUL BIEGEL

'Listen!'

In the ancient city of Dippity-Dong there lived a mouse who very much wanted to move to the city of Sippity-Song since he had a rather good baritone voice. So he hopped into the pocket of a passing soldier who was marching to the barracks at Lippity-Long. When they arrived the mouse scuttled into the general's boot which was being taken to the cobbler. But the cobbler lived at Hippity-Hong, so the mouse had to skip out and hide in a bag that lay on a handcart.

The handcart was pushed to Crippity-Crong, and here the mouse hurriedly leapt on top of a hat that a man was just putting on.

The man mounted his horse and galloped away. He was indeed going to Sippity-Song, but as he was crossing a bridge over the river, the mouse was blown off by a gust of wind and fell into a boat that carried him on to Prippity Prong instead.

Now here in the doctor's house, lived the mouse's niece. He knocked at the door of her home.

'Who's there?' called the niece.

'Me!' cried the mouse.

'How did you get here?' asked the niece.

'By soldier, boot, cart, horse and boat,' the mouse said. 'I'm on my way to Sippity-Song.'

'Sing to me,' said the niece.

The mouse then sang the Song of the Grey Tail, and the Four Skippy Legs song, while the niece, in her soprano voice, joined in.

The mouse stayed two days. They ate the doctor's cheese, and during the night they sang and danced on the table laid for breakfast. Hup-two, hip-two, over the jam pot and the syrup pot and the honey pot. Afterwards they slept in the doctor's napkin as though it were a bed with white sheets.

Then the mouse wanted to be on his way again.

'How will you get to Sippity-Song?' asked the niece.

'By doctor's black bag,' said the mouse.

He kissed her good-bye, and slipped into the bag which lay open beside the front door.

The doctor had seven patients to visit. The first one lay ill at Prippity-Prong, the second lay ill at Sippity-Song.

'Out!' thought the mouse. But his tail became entangled with the stethoscope, and before he could free himself the doctor had cured the patient and snapped the bag tight.

The next four patients lived in quite different cities. The last patient was a very long ride away.

'I just have to stay where I am,' thought the mouse.

When the doctor opened his bag and took out his stethoscope, the mouse still had his tail caught in it, and before he could disentangle it there he hung, in mid-air. Then he leapt over the patient and scampered out of the house. And where did he find himself but in his own ancient city of Dippity-Dong!

Back at home he altered the sign on the door of his hole. 'J. Mouse, baritone' was scratched out and painted over in beautiful lettering: J. MOUSE. ROUND-THE-WORLD EXPLORER.

From *The King of the Copper Mountains*

The Little Storm

RUDOLF NEUMANN

It was the Sun's turn to shine on Sunday. On Monday the East Wind went out. On Tuesday, long before daybreak, St Peter was driving his sheep, the grey clouds, out of their fold.

The Little Storm kept grumbling and muttering to itself.

'When can I have a turn?' it asked impatiently.

'Well – maybe next Thursday!' said St Peter, smiling.

Sure enough, first thing on Thursday St Peter unbarred the gates of Heaven and let the Little Storm out.

Down went the Little Storm to earth, rushing and roaring. 'And who might you be?' inquired the weather-cock on the steeple in surprise.

'I'm the Little Storm! Come on, let's play a game!' And it seized the weathercock and whirled it around, faster and faster, until it was quite dizzy.

'Stop, stop!' screeched the poor weathercock. But the Little Storm was off again. There were nine oleander trees growing in brightly painted tubs outside the café in the market place. They stood there bolt upright, one behind the other. *Whoosh!* – the Little Storm rushed up to them. Three, five, seven, eight, nine – they were all bowled over! The Little Storm was off again.

There was an empty sardine tin lying in the gutter in St Martin's Row. It had been there for days. It must have dropped out of the dust cart. *Whoosh!* Up swept the Little Storm. How that can rattled! *Ping!* It hit the wall on the right. *Ping!* It hit the wall on the left. Then it shot through a gateway.

The Little Storm shot through the gateway too, and came
to a garden where there was washing hanging on the line.
'Ha, ha, ha!' chuckled the Little Storm, tearing an apron
off the line. Just then a woman came with a laundry basket.
'Good gracious, where's my apron?' she thought in alarm,
looking around for it. Where indeed? Why, it was right up
in the plum tree, on the very top branch! But the Little
Storm was off again.

'What weather!' thought the Mayor, coming out of the
Town Hall. 'What shocking weather!' *Whee!* The Little
Storm came roaring up and tore the Mayor's hat from his
head with one gust.

'What weather!' thought the burglar, creeping up to an
empty house. He had spied it out before; the people who
lived there were all away on holiday. 'What wonderful

weather,' thought the burglar, 'no one will hear a window pane break in this.' And he smashed in the glass.

'What weather!' thought the policeman standing in Station Road to direct the traffic. However, there was no traffic to direct in this weather; everyone was staying at home. Ah, here comes a hat, though. The policeman spread his arms wide to hold it up, but it was not the slightest use. The hat took no notice of him at all.

'Stop!' shouted the policeman angrily.

'Stop!' Was it an echo? No, it was the Mayor just turning the corner. 'Catch that hat!' he shouted.

'Ho, ho, ho!' laughed the Little Storm, dancing along with the hat – one, two three, hop! The policeman ran after the hat, the Mayor ran after the policeman. But when they all stopped running and dancing, lo and behold, they were standing outside a house with a window open. The glass was broken.

'What's all this?' said the Mayor.

'What's all this?' said the policeman.

And last of all – 'What's all this?' said the burglar. He was just climbing out of the window with his loot when, much to his surprise, he felt two strong hands grab him.

'*Whooooo!*' howled the Little Storm and away it blew.

Then all of a sudden it noticed how terribly tired it was. It whistled quickly around a couple of corners, but it wasn't such fun any more. It began to yawn, '*Aaaaaah!*'

'What, as tired as all that?' asked a voice. It sounded familiar. And when the Little Storm looked up, it saw the Sun pushing the grey clouds aside and beaming down cheerfully.

'Come along, home you go,' said the Sun.

Then the Little Storm took one jump and hopped up on to one of the clouds, and back it flew to the sky. St Peter was standing outside the gates of Heaven. 'Well?' he asked. 'How was it?'

'Wonderful!' sighed the Little Storm happily. 'I played whipping tops with the weathercock and I played ninepins with the oleander trees. I played football with the sardine tin and hide-and-seek with the apron. I played tag with the Mayor's hat and I played cops-and-robbers. *Aaaaaah!*'

It snuggled down into its soft grey cloud, half asleep already, but murmuring 'When can I do it again?'

'Next Thursday, maybe,' said St Peter smiling. 'We'll have to see.' And he closed the gates of Heaven.

From *The Kind Crocodile*

The Wind

JAMES REEVES

I can get through a doorway without any key,
And strip the leaves from the great oak tree.

I can drive storm-clouds and shake tall towers,
Or steal through a garden and not wake the flowers.

Seas I can move and ships I can sink;
I can carry a house-top or the scent of a pink.

When I am angry I can rave and riot,
And when I am spent, I lie quiet as quiet.

From *The Wandering Moon*

The Magic Pencil

CHARLOTTE HOUGH

One day when Annabel was throwing sticks for her dog in the woods near her home she found a magic pencil in the bracken. She knew it was magic because when she happened to draw a cat with it in her drawing-book that evening the drawing faded away from the page and a dear little real tabby cat appeared instead and settled itself down on the mat in front of the fire. So then Annabel drew a saucer of cream and that appeared too and the little cat lapped it up with a proper little real pink tongue.

After that Annabel's mother called her down to supper and she hadn't really got a chance to be by herself again until the next day after breakfast. It was nearly Christmas time, so Annabel went up to her bedroom and drew a fur coat for her mother and hung it up at the back of her wardrobe so that it would be a secret. Then she drew a motor-car for her father and she looked out of the window and saw it come purring up to the front door all by itself. It was rather an old-fashioned one because that was the only sort that Annabel knew how to draw, but it was beautifully black and shiny with red leather seats and a big rubber horn. Then Annabel drew the car again, but all hidden by trees this time, and she looked out of the window and watched while it started itself up and drove itself into the woods so that it should be a secret.

Then Annabel got very excited and she was just about to draw a lot more things when she heard her mother calling her from downstairs asking her to take the dog out for a walk because it was a nice day and her mother thought it might cloud over later on.

So Annabel, who was a good obedient child, put her drawing-book away in a drawer and took the dog out for a walk in the woods and when she reached the place where she had found the pencil there was a goblin with a very worried expression on his face, walking round and round in circles looking for something.

As soon as Annabel saw him she guessed that he was looking for the magic pencil, but when the goblin asked her if she had seen it Annabel said 'No,' and added under her breath 'not before yesterday', so that it would not be quite so untrue, but not so that the goblin could hear her.

The goblin looked so disappointed that Annabel felt sorry for him, but all the same she couldn't bear to give it back to him before she had drawn some presents for herself. So she said she was in rather a hurry and she called her dog and ran back home as quickly as she could and she went up to her bedroom and drew herself a big box of chocolates and ate them nearly all. Then she drew a picture of herself

with very thick eyelashes and long hair which came right
down below her waist, and a beautiful party frock which was
a proper long grown-up one with a sash which tied in a bow,
and when she looked at herself in the mirror she looked so
pretty that she could hardly believe it.

Then Annabel thought she would have a party to go with
the party frock and she thought what fun it would be to
draw all the things she liked best at parties: crackers and
prizes and cakes and trifles and balloons and ices and little
baby sausages and sandwiches and flags sticking out of
them to say what they were. But the more Annabel thought
about these things the more she thought that she would do

it in a little while but not yet, because she had eaten so many chocolates just lately, so she decided to go and call on her friend Jane and show her the dress and the eyelashes and the hair and perhaps let her do one little drawing for herself with the pencil.

Jane lived in a house on the other side of the wood, and when Annabel came to the part where the goblin was she looked the other way because it made her feel so guilty to see him looking for his pencil.

But the goblin saw her and he called out: 'That's a fine new party dress you've got on today.'

'Yes,' said Annabel, turning round. 'My mother made it,' and she added under her breath, 'my breakfast, I mean,' so as to make it be not quite so untrue, but she went rather red.

But as soon as the goblin saw her face he realized that her hair and her eyelashes were quite different from yesterday and that she must have got hold of some magic because she was quite an ordinary little girl and not a fairy, and he shouted out in a terrible voice: 'YOU'VE GOT MY PENCIL!' and he started to run after her and Annabel started to run away because she was frightened of the goblin when he was so angry even though he was smaller than she was. But she couldn't run nearly as fast as usual because her dress was so long it kept catching in the branches and she couldn't see properly because she had so many eyelashes, and presently she fell flat on her face and the magic pencil rolled out of her pocket and the goblin pounced on it and picked it up. He pointed it at her and shouted at once:

'Magic pencil take away
The things she's drawn for herself today!'

Then the goblin ran off into the bracken clutching his pencil and leaving Annabel sitting there in her vest and knickers, with her ordinary hair and ordinary eyelashes.

When she got home her mother was very cross with her for going out of doors in her underclothes. When Annabel tried to explain about the goblin and the magic pencil her mother wouldn't believe her and said she must have been dreaming, and when Annabel showed her the tabby kitten she said it must be a little stray cat who had come in through the window.

But Annabel knew she hadn't been dreaming, because why should she have been feeling so sick if she hadn't just eaten nearly a whole box of chocolates?

And *they'll* know, won't they, on the 25th December!

From *Charlotte Hough's Holiday Book*

The Tortoises' Picnic

ANON

There were once three tortoises – a father, a mother, and a baby. And one fine spring day they decided that they would like to go for a picnic. They picked the place they would go to, a nice wood at some distance off, and they began to get their stuff together. They got tins of salmon and tins of tongue, and sandwiches, and orange squash and everything they could think of. In about three months they were ready, and they set out, carrying their baskets.

They walked and walked and walked, and time went on, and after about eighteen months they sat down and had a rest. But they knew just where they wanted to go and they were about halfway to it, so they set out again. And in three years they reached the picnic place. They unpacked their baskets and spread out the cloth, and arranged the food on it and it looked lovely.

Then Mother Tortoise began to look into the picnic baskets. She turned them all upside down, and shook them, but they were all empty and at last she said, 'We've forgotten the tin-opener!' They looked at each other, and at last Father and Mother Tortoise said, 'Baby, you'll have to go back for it.' 'What!' said the baby. 'Me! Go back all that long way!' 'Nothing for it,' said Father Tortoise, 'we can't start without a tin-opener. We'll wait for you.' 'Well, do you swear, do you promise faithfully that you won't touch a thing till I come back?' said the baby. 'Yes, we promise faithfully,' they said and Baby plodded away, and after a while he was lost to sight amongst the bushes.

And Father and Mother Tortoise waited. They waited and waited and waited and a whole year went by, and they began to get rather hungry. But they'd promised, so they waited. And another year went by, and another, and they got really hungry. 'Don't you think we could have just one sandwich each?' asked Mother Tortoise. 'He'd never know the difference.' 'No,' said Father Tortoise, 'we promised. We must wait till Baby comes back.'

So they waited and another year passed, and another, and they got ravenous. 'It's six years now,' said Mother Tortoise. 'He ought to be back by now.'

'Yes, I suppose he ought,' said Father Tortoise. 'Let's just have one sandwich while we're waiting.'

They picked up the sandwiches, but just as they were going to eat them, a little voice said, 'Aha! I knew you'd cheat,' and Baby Tortoise popped his head out of a bush. 'It's a good thing I didn't start at all for that tin-opener!' he said.

From *A Dictionary of British Folk Tales*

Everything's Horrid Today

ANN STADON

George had just had a birthday – it had been such a lovely day. Grandma had sent him a set of farmyard toys – a tractor, a combine harvester, a plough and a truck – and Auntie had given him a book of stories that George hadn't seen before. Six of his friends had come to tea, and they had eaten crisps, sausages on sticks and ice-cream, and had balloons to play with afterwards. But the very best thing was the tent that Mother and Father had given him, a real tent, not a play tent, a tent that you could really sleep in.

George's birthday had been on a Friday, so, as Father had to go to work, and Mother was so busy making things for the party, Father promised that they would put up the tent for the first time on Saturday. George didn't mind waiting for just one more day, because he had his farm toys to play with and his new book to look at, and his party to look forward to.

But on Saturday morning when George woke up, the first thing he heard was the steady drip-drip of rain on his window-pane. He got out of bed and went over to the window. The sky looked grey and heavy, the sort of sky that tells you that it will rain all day. George knew at once that he wouldn't be able to put up his tent in the rain.

'Bother!' he said. 'Bother! I know everything's going to be horrid today.'

At breakfast time he sulked and grunted and wouldn't eat his toast because he said it was burnt. 'Don't be in such a state, old fellow,' said Father. 'It may clear up later.'

When George turned to look out of the window to see if it would clear up, he knocked his milk over, and the milky puddle spread right across the table and began to drip on the floor. Mother was cross and said he was a naughty, careless boy, which made George more miserable than ever.

'Everything's horrid today!' he said.

After breakfast he played with his farm toys again, but it didn't seem half as much fun as yesterday. He ran over the cat's tail with his harvester, and the cat scratched him not very hard, but it made George cry.

Father suggested that they played snakes and ladders for a while. That was fun . . . until George had to go right down the biggest snake to number five, and Father won the game.

'It's your unlucky day,' said Father. 'Never mind. Have a sweet for a consolation prize. That will make you feel better.' He handed George a red fruit drop, his very favourite. But, would you believe it, George swallowed it whole, quite without meaning to. It did hurt his tummy.

'Horrid, horrid, day!' he sobbed.

At dinner-time there was a big pot of stew, with butter

beans and carrots in it. 'Horrid butter beans!' said George. 'I hate butter beans.'

'George,' said Mother, 'I have had enough. Go to your bedroom until you can be a bit more cheerful.'

George stomped upstairs and slammed the bedroom door with a great big bang. The draught made all the birthday cards, which he had so carefully arranged on his dressing-table, blow over. Half of them fell on the floor, and two went behind the dressing-table, where he couldn't reach them.

Poor George – Father heard him crying and came up-stairs. He picked up all the cards, even the two behind the dressing-table, and then he took George on his lap. 'Now, old fellow,' he said. 'Shall I tell you what I think is the matter? I think you got out of bed on the wrong side this morning. The thing to do is to go back to bed, just for half an hour, and try getting up again.'

'Don't want to go to bed,' said George. 'I'm a big boy now I've had my birthday.'

'Well,' said Father, 'it's up to you. But I think it would be a very interesting experiment. We could find out whether there is a right and wrong side of bed.'

Father took off George's slippers and pullover and tucked him up in bed. 'I'll read you a story from your new book,' he suggested. 'Which one shall it be?'

George chose the longest story in the book, about an Eskimo boy who lived in an igloo near the North Pole. Father sat on the edge of the bed and read it all through. George hadn't thought he was in the least bit tired, but he fell asleep just as Father was closing the book.

He slept for two whole hours, but it seemed only five

minutes to George before Father was gently shaking his shoulders and saying, 'Wake up, George. Wake up.'

As soon as George opened his eyes, he knew that everything was different. It wasn't a horrid day after all. The sunlight was so bright that it made him blink.

'Come on, George,' said Father. 'Come and give me a hand with the tent.'

George jumped out of bed, on the right side this time, and they went out into the garden.

It was a lovely tent, blue and orange, with a door in front which zipped open and shut, and a little window made of net. Mother let Father and George have tea in the tent, and, as George had had such a good sleep in the afternoon, he was allowed to stay up for a bit in the evening. They all played snakes and ladders again and guess who won this time . . . George, of course!

'There,' said Father as he said good-night. 'It hasn't been such a horrid day after all, has it?'

George thought for a moment, and then he said, 'No, it wasn't a horrid day at all. I think it was just me who was horrid.'

What do you think?

From *Pepper Face and Other Stories*

If I were a Fish

ALISON WINN

Splash, splosh!
Whenever I wash
I wish and wish and wish
That I lived in the water all day long
Like a slithery, slippery fish.

Splash, splish!
If I were a fish
I wouldn't have to wash.
I wouldn't need soap or a towel or a sponge,
But I'd splish –
    And I'd splash –
        And I'd splosh!

From *Swings and Things*

Bertha Gets into Trouble:

The Story of a Tanker Ship

LIANE SMITH

The fat old tanker ship, Bertha, was not feeling very well. She had just finished a very nasty job. Instead of the petrol she usually carried in her tanks, she had had to carry some horrid thick black oil to a country far across the ocean. This country had been especially short of thick black oil, but had had plenty of petrol. Now that Bertha had finished her job, she was not happy at all. Her shiny green decks were all smeary and slippery with horrid thick black oil, and her tanks felt all sticky.

'Ugh!' she said – only it didn't come out as 'Ugh!', of course, but as 'Pah-rump!'. 'My tanks feel so nasty, and I look *such* a mess! Just suppose any of my friends were to see me now – how ashamed I should feel!' And she blew such a lot of smoke out of her funnel, that it billowed all round her in a big cloud, and sat gently on her decks, until you could hardly see Bertha at all. 'I shall hide behind this smoke cloud,' she said to herself, 'until someone comes to make me look smart again.' And then she was quite quiet.

'Cheer up, Bertha,' said her Captain. 'We'll soon have you ship-shape again. You'll feel a different ship after a good hose down and tank clean.' Bertha thought that sounded hopeful, but she still didn't say anything. She was feeling just a little sulky.

The sailors worked very hard, and soon Bertha's decks were free of all the sticky black oil, and were shiny and green again.

'That's a bit better,' said Bertha to herself. 'But I shan't feel right until all that nasty treacly oil is out of my tanks.'

Soon, she felt a *swish, swish* and a *slosh, slosh, slosh* going on in her tanks. *Swish, swish, slosh, swoosh* the feeling went, and Bertha began to feel much less cross.

When the swishing and the sloshing had quite finished, Bertha said to herself: 'Now that the sailors have finished, I can get rid of all the dirty oily water in my tanks. Good!' And she gave a loud 'Paarmp! Paarmp!' of relief, and opened the pipes that led out of her tanks, to let the dirty, oily water swoosh out into the deep greeny sea.

Then Bertha had a shock. 'Mee-ew! Mee-ew!' It was a loud angry noise, and it came from the top of her funnel . . . 'I know that voice,' said Bertha to herself. 'That's my friend Gully, the seagull. Hello, Gully, how nice of you

to call. I *am* pleased to see you. It's a good job you didn't come a bit earlier. You would have found me in a dreadful sticky state.'

'Well, just take a good look at me, then,' said Gully, and he didn't sound *at all* pleased to see Bertha. And when Bertha had a good look at Gully, she had a great shock. She hardly knew him! His feathers, usually sleek and white, were smeared with black streaks, and his wings wouldn't spread out properly, they were so sticky.

He looked something like Bertha had looked a little while before, except that it is rather difficult for a small seagull to look like a big tanker ship.

'Wherever have you been, Gully?' asked Bertha.

'Can't you guess?' said Gully. And then Bertha began to think. She thought of the sticky black oil, and the water in her tanks going *swish*, *swosh*, and of the dirty oily water going into the sea, and she knew that Gully had been in that dirty oil water.

'Yes, Gully,' Bertha said, in a very small voice. 'I can guess – and I am terribly sorry.'

'So you should be,' said Gully. He *was* cross. 'I was just diving for a quick fish snack, and when I came up, I was in a thick oily patch of sea, instead of the nice clear green water I dived into. Just look behind you!'

And Bertha looked, and saw a long purple-black line stretching a long, long way behind her.

'Oh, dear!' said Bertha.

'Yes – oh, dear!' said Gully. 'I was lucky – I managed to hop out of the water quickly. If I had been in any longer my wings wouldn't have worked any more, and *then* where would I have been?' Then he turned his back on Bertha,

and began combing through his dirty feathers with his orange beak.

Now Bertha felt very ashamed – much more so than if Gully had seen her when *she* was all oily.

She cleared her funnel. 'Prrrump. I am very, very sorry indeed, Gully, to have been so thoughtless. In future I shall put all my dirty washing-water into one tank, and keep it until I find the proper place to let it out.' And Bertha remembered that the pipes were still letting oily water out into the sea, so she shut them quickly. 'Please, Gully, will you forgive me, so that we can be friends again?'

Now Gully was very fond of Bertha, and he was a good-tempered seagull, as seagulls go – and besides, his feathers were clean again now, after his hard work. So he said 'Mee-ew! I don't see why not – let's be friends again.'

And so they were and Bertha never again let her dirty oily water into the sea in places where the seagulls might get hurt.

From *Bertha the Tanker*

Michael and the Bird

CATHERINE MASON (*aged* 7)

Once upon a time there was a terrible little boy and his name was Michael. Michael was in his garden when he thought he would go for a walk. So off he went along the green lanes until he came to a little tree and at one side of the tree there was a bush. There he saw a little nest. 'Oh,' he said, 'the mother wouldn't mind if I take one egg. After all she is being greedy having four and even three is quite greedy.' So he took the fourth egg and put it in his pocket.

Suddenly he heard a voice saying, 'Where is my fourth egg?' He felt for the egg and it was still there. He put his handkerchief over it and went on. But the bird saw him and said, 'Hello, have you seen my fourth egg?' 'No,' said Michael. 'I expect a cuckoo has pushed it out and is coming back to lay her eggs.' 'Oh dear!' said the bird. 'I have visitors tomorrow.' 'Well, you'll just have to show them another nest,' said Michael and he started to go away.

'Stop, oh, please stop,' said the bird. 'Will you help me please, little boy?' 'I hope I can help you,' said Michael. 'Shush!' said the bird, 'you might wake them up.' 'What and who are *they*?' asked Michael. 'My babies,' said the bird. 'Are they alive?' asked Michael. 'Yes,' answered the bird, 'but you can't see them because they are alive inside the eggs. Maybe you can see them tomorrow because they might have hatched out then, but I don't think so because I just laid them yesterday. I am going to try very hard because last year they didn't hatch out and I do want some babies of my own, and it is a pity not to have company, isn't it?' 'I suppose so,' said Michael, 'anyway, how can I help you?'

'Well,' said the bird, 'I told the visitors that I had seven eggs and now I only have three because the cuckoo stole four eggs and has not come to lay her own eggs. All you have to do is to make four eggs for me.' 'How can I make eggs?' said Michael. 'Well, you get some plasticine or clay and you make it into the shape of an egg and then you paint them blue with black spots on, and then you put them to dry and when they are dry you can put them in my nest and then the visitors will think they are my eggs. All right?' 'Yes,' said Michael, 'all right.' 'Well, get to work then. There is some clay outside the pot factory over there.'

So off went Michael and got a lot of clay, some blue paint and black paint and went back to the bird. 'Now make it into the shape of an egg,' said the bird. 'Yes, that's right . . . now paint it blue . . . very good . . . and put black spots on it . . . right, put it to dry in the sun. We can make three more and put them all in that place and when they are dry, we can put them in my nest.' And while the bird sat on the real eggs, Michael made the toy eggs. He thought it was great fun because he liked getting dirty, but his father and mother did not let him usually. He painted his fingers, his face and his arms and got very dirty indeed. 'My goodness me,' said the bird. 'If I had known you were as naughty as that, painting yourself all over, I would have done the job myself. Still I suppose you have tried very hard but you needn't have painted yourself all over, need you?' 'I suppose not,' said Michael, 'but I can wash myself in that stream over there.' 'Well, go and wash yourself, little boy.' 'Oh, I wish you would stop calling me "little boy"', said Michael. 'What shall I call you then?' 'Michael is my name and my other name is David. I have another name too, it is Stephen, but I would rather you called me Michael, please.'

'Well, Michael, come and visit me again when you have had your walk,' said the bird. 'Oh, I would like to stay with you instead of going on a walk. I like you,' said Michael. 'I like you better than my mother and father because they are always scolding me for nothing and I always apologize to them. You know, I wouldn't be naughty on purpose, would I?' 'I know, I get in a temper myself sometimes,' said the bird.

'I am glad that you like me,' said the bird, 'because one day I held a meeting and I asked everybody what two and three was and none of the birds knew except me and my cousins (because I told them before that it made 'Five') and the other birds found out that I had told my cousins so they do not like me any more. I have nineteen cousins that live near me and lots of other relations too. The visitors who are coming are my cousins from India. They are staying with me in this nest but I do not know how to fit us all into my nest because it is very small.' 'Well,' said Michael, 'you could make another nest which you could use when you have babies as well as using it for visitors.' 'That's a good idea,' said the bird. 'Please will you get some twigs from the wood.' 'Yes,' said Michael, 'I will get some mud and earth and grass and straw as well.'

'I would like you to call me Jenny,' said the bird. 'I know it isn't really a bird's name, but I chose it because it was very nice, but you can call me Miss Pip or anything at all except rude names.' 'Well, I will call you Mrs Bird,' said Michael. 'That is a nice name,' said the bird, 'birds don't usually have names, do they?' 'No,' agreed Michael, 'anyway not wild birds, but maybe pet birds, then their owner will always have the same bird if he calls it back after a fly in the woods.' 'But I am not a pet bird,' said Mrs Bird, 'so my mother and father did not christen me. Anyway, are those toy eggs dry yet?' 'No, but they soon will be, but the sun has gone in now. Shall I put them in another sunny place?' 'I want them in my nest as soon as possible,' said the bird, 'because the visitors said they might arrive a bit earlier than tomorrow. You see they are very fast flyers, much faster than me because they have a lot of exercise and I don't. But they have got some babies that have just learnt how to fly and the babies might not be able to go very fast so they might arrive tomorrow afternoon.'

'Oh, I bet I could beat them if I was running my fastest,' said Michael. 'No, you could not,' said the bird, 'they are much too fast for you to catch up. Are the eggs ready?' 'Yes,' said Michael and he put them in the bird's nest. 'You have been so helpful, I don't know how to reward you,' said Mrs Bird. 'Well,' said Michael, 'you might as well throw one toy egg away because I took one of your real eggs and here you are, you can have it back.' 'Oh,' said the bird, 'was it you who took my fourth egg?' 'Yes,' said Michael, 'it was me and I shouldn't have taken it, it was not my property, so here,' and Michael gave the egg to the bird. 'I must go now and I hope you have a nice time when your cousins come, good-bye.'

He went down by the stream and right back to his garden where he had started his walk.

Mr and Mrs Spikky Sparrow

EDWARD LEAR

On a little piece of wood,
Mr Spikky Sparrow stood;

Mrs Sparrow sat close by,
A-making of an insect pie,

For her little children five
In the nest and all alive,

Singing with a cheerful smile,
To amuse them all the while,

'Twikky wikky wikky we,
Wikky bikky twikky tee,
Spikky bikky bee!'

The Invitation

RICHARD HUGHES

There was once a little girl who slept in a very large room all alone. Sometimes she woke up in the night, and then she would feel very dull at having nothing to do except go to sleep again. So one night when she woke up, she sat up in bed and looked at the moonlight coming in at the window. While she was doing that there was a sudden *Pop!* and the top button of her pyjamas flew off. But instead of falling on the bed, it floated gently across the room and out of the window; and once it was out of the window, it stuck in the air, almost within reach. So the little girl got out of bed and went to the window to try and get it back. But, try as she would, she just couldn't reach it. So she climbed on to the windowsill to try and reach further, and in doing so she tumbled right out.

Don't you try!

When she had floated slowly down to the ground she looked about her, but the button was nowhere to be seen. Only the moonlight shone through the trees of the drive and the wind rustled gently through their leaves. For a minute she stood wondering what to do; and then she heard steps coming up the drive, so she hid behind a tree to see who it was. What was her surprise when the steps passed her, and she couldn't see anything at all! Only a postman's cap that floated along about the height of a man's head.

'Well,' she thought very sensibly, 'I suppose this post-man is invisible, and has an invisible uniform, but he has taken another postman's cap by mistake.'

So she stepped out into the moonlight, where he could see her, and asked if he had any letters for her.

'Yes,' he said, 'here is one' and putting into her hand an invisible letter he walked away down the drive.

Of course the trouble is with an invisible letter that you can't read it, so the little girl was rather worried what to do. At last she decided she would go and see her very best friend, who was one of the gateposts down at the end of the drive. So holding the letter very tight (because if she dropped it she would never be able to find it again), she walked down the drive after the postman and climbed on to her friend.

'Dear gatepost,' she said, 'do help me to read this letter.'

And immediately the letter became visible, and she read it.

'*Dear little girl*,' it said, '*we are giving a party in our castle tonight. Will you come?*'

That was all: it didn't say who it was from, or where the castle was or anything. Now the little girl knew the country around well, and there wasn't any castle there anywhere. That is to say, at any rate there were none on the ground; there might be some in the air – that she didn't know. So she climbed a tall tree to have a look.

At the top of the tree there was a railway station, with a train just going to start: so she got in, and away the train went across the sky till it came to another station, and there she got out.

'Can you please tell me the way to the castle?' she said to the station-master.

'Which castle?' he asked. 'There are nine near this station.'

So she showed him the letter. He scratched his head.

'Well,' he said, 'that's the queerest letter I have ever seen, so I expect it comes from the queerest castle. And *that* one is only just round the corner.'

So he told her where to go and she soon came to it.

It was indeed the queerest of all castles, for it was upside down.

The gate was at the top, with big towers below it, and a flag at the bottom.

'Well,' she thought, 'I suppose that the best way to get in is to turn upside down too.'

So she did, and soon found herself walking in at the gate quite comfortably.

The party that was going on in the big hall inside was simply lovely. Each person was dressed all in one colour, and these colours were of the brightest. There would be one person in bright lilac, and another in blue, and another in peacock, and another in green, and another in yellow, and another in orange, and another in scarlet, and another in crimson. They all nodded to the little girl and told her they were glad she had come. The ones who were talking walked about the floor, but if they wanted to dance they did it on the ceiling, where there was more room, and if they wanted something to eat they walked up the walls to little tables which stuck out here and there.

Presently the little girl found a nice man to dance with, so they went up to the ceiling and danced round and round the electric light. Then they walked down the wall to one of the little tables and there ate ices.

'What will you do,' he asked presently, 'when the Special Licence gives way?'

'What is the Special Licence?' asked the little girl.

'It is a sort of spell,' he said, 'giving leave to the castle to be upside down. And it gives way at one o'clock – why it's nearly one o'clock now.'

'Oh, I'll wait and see what happens,' said the little girl very sensibly, and began hurriedly to eat another ice before the time should be up.

When it struck one, the first thing that happened was that all the people shrank and turned into mice; but they still stayed their lovely colours, and chased each other round and round the little girl, looking very pretty. Next the castle got smaller and smaller, and finally came to bits till there was nothing left but a single bit of broken china; and the mice all ran away.

'Thank you very much,' she called after them: 'I *did* enjoy myself.'

Then the little girl found she was at home, and sitting under the kitchen table.

So she stole quietly up to bed again, and luckily no one heard her.

From *The Wonder Dog*

The Farmer and the Pixie

A Story from Devonshire

There was once a young farmer who lived in Devon. His farm was small and the land was not very good, so he could afford only one man to help him. The farmer worked hard but he didn't seem to have much luck.

One day he got up early and went to plough a distant field. He hadn't been there long when his man came running and shouted, 'Master! Master! There's a little old man in the barn – about this high – and he's threshing the wheat. He don't say nothing but he's working terrible hard. I reckon he's a pixie and that's good luck!'

The farmer left his man to get on with the ploughing and hurried to the barn. No one there! But in the middle of the floor was a pile of corn and the barn was swept.

The young man went into the house to tell his wife what had happened. 'Maybe we'll have better luck now,' he said. 'But I doubt the little man will come again – our farm is so poor.'

He was so sure that the pixie would not be seen again that he went to the barn in good time the next day to get on with the threshing. There was nothing for him to do. The corn had been threshed already, the barn was tidy. The pixie had swept away the chaff and the dust.

'Well, that is good luck!' said the farmer, well pleased. 'I must see the little man who is doing me this good turn. Tonight I'll watch for him and thank him. Then maybe he'll come again.'

So that night he had his supper late, then sat by the warm
fire and tried to keep awake. The fire burnt low, the grand-
father clock ticked in the corner, a mouse ran out and picked
up the crumbs under the kitchen table. But the farmer saw
and heard nothing for he was fast asleep and snoring. He
had been in the open air all day and he couldn't keep his
eyes open. When he wakened it was morning and although
he hurried out to the barn, it was empty. But the pile of
corn was there and the barn had been swept.

This happened several nights, so the farmer made a
different plan. He had his supper early and fell asleep at
once. At midnight his alarm clock whirred and woke him.
He jumped out of bed, scrambled into his clothes and hurried to the barn. There was no one there so he hid in the
straw and waited. He wasn't likely to fall asleep again for the
straw tickled him so.

For a time nothing happened and the farmer was afraid

the pixie wasn't coming at all. Then, just before daybreak, there was a rustling in the corner of the barn and out came a little man only a foot high. He had bright twinkling eyes, a brown skin and ragged clothes, reddish brown like Devonshire soil.

The little man spread out the wheat, beat it with his flail, then made a pile of the corn in the middle of the barn. He tied the straw into neat bundles and swept the floor. He worked so hard and so quickly that the dust flew everywhere and got into the farmer's eyes. When he could see again, the pixie was gone. He searched the barn but there was no sign of the little man.

The farmer went into the warm farmhouse to have his breakfast of bacon and eggs. 'The pixie has come again, wife,' he said. 'He works hard does that little man. We really ought to pay him but human money is no good to fairy folk.'

'Is there anything he needs, do you think?' asked his wife.

The farmer laughed. 'I reckon he needs some new clothes,' he said. 'You can see daylight through those he has, they are so full of holes.'

'Then I'll make him some new ones,' said his wife. 'How big is he?'

'Oh, about as high as that chair leg,' said the farmer, 'but quite fat.'

When she had fed the hens and made the butter, the farmer's wife went to her piece bag and hunted out all the brightly coloured bits of material she had. There was a piece of red velvet big enough to make trousers for the little man. A piece of white linen would make him a shirt, but what about a coat? Here was a fine piece of blue silk that would just do. Last of all she found a tiny piece of bright yellow felt for a cap.

The farmer's wife was clever with her needle. All day she cut and snipped, hemmed and stitched. By evening she had made a tiny pair of red breeches, a white shirt with a ruffle down the front, a handsome blue silk coat and a perky yellow cap. When she showed them to her husband, he thought they were very smart and laughed to think how pleased the pixie would be.

At night he did as before – he slept first, then woke and crept out to the barn. He placed the new suit in the middle of the floor, just where the first rays of the sun would strike it. Even in the light of his lantern, it looked gay and colourful. The farmer hid himself as before.

Sure enough, just before cockcrow, the little man crept out of a corner and began to thresh the wheat. It was not until the first rays of the sun lit up the barn that he caught sight of the little suit.

He picked up the red breeches, the blue coat, the white shirt and the yellow cap in turn and held them up against himself with delight. Then he laid them down carefully and clapped his hands in excitement. Round and round the barn he pranced, stamping his feet, his ragged clothes fluttering round him.

'For me!' he sang. 'For me! Oh, lucky me! Lucky me!'

At last, out of breath, he stopped and dressed himself in the new clothes – the fine red breeches, the snow-white shirt, the handsome blue coat. Last of all he perched the tiny yellow cap on his head.

There was a shallow pool of water in one corner of the

barn where a broken slate had let the rain through. The little man peered into it to see what he looked like. 'How smart I am!' he cried. 'No more work for me! I might spoil my new suit!'

He capered about so fast that the dust flew into the farmer's face and he sneezed several times. When he looked again, the little man had disappeared. Only his old rags were blowing about the dusty floor.

The farmer never saw the pixie again, but from that day he had better luck. His crops were good and he made money, two fine sons were born to him who soon helped him on the farm and, what is more, he was a happy man ever afterwards.

The Little Market Woman

TRADITIONAL

There was a little woman,
  As I've heard tell,
She went to market
  Her eggs for to sell,
She went to market
  All on a market day,
And she fell asleep
  On the King's highway.

There came a pedlar
  His name was Stout,
He cut her petticoats
  All round about;
He cut her petticoats
  Up to her knees,
Which made the poor woman
  To shiver and sneeze.

When the little woman
  Began to awake,
She began to shiver,
  And she began to shake;
She began to shake,
  And she began to cry,
Goodness mercy on me,
  This is none of I!

If it be not I
   As I suppose it be,
I have a little dog at home,
   And he knows me;
If it be I,
   He'll wag his little tail,
And if it be not I,
   He'll loudly bark and wail.

Home went the little woman,
   All in the dark,
Up jumped the little dog,
   And he began to bark,
He began to bark,
   And she began to cry,
Goodness mercy on me,
   I see I be not I!

This poor little woman
　Passed the night on a stile,
She shivered with cold,
　And she trembled the while:
She slept not a wink
　But was all night awake,
And was heartily glad
　When the morning did break.

There came by the pedlar
　Returning from town,
She asked him for something
　To match her short gown,
The sly pedlar rogue
　Showed the piece he'd purloined,
Said to the woman,
　It will do nicely joined.

She pinned on the piece,
　And exclaimed What a match!
I am lucky indeed
　Such a bargain to catch.
The dog wagged his tail,
　And she began to cry,
Goodness mercy on me,
　I've discovered it be I!

How Puss and Pup Made a Birthday Cake

JOSEPH CAPEK

One day Puss said to Pup, 'Look here, it's our birthday to-morrow, we ought to make ourselves a cake! The only thing is I don't know how to.'

'Oh, it's easy,' said Pup. 'I know the way to make a proper cake! You just put in all the best things there are, everything you like eating best of all, and then's the cake the best you could want.'

'Yes, you're quite right,' said Puss. 'We'll make the best cake there can possibly be.'

Puss and Pup put on their aprons and started cooking.

First they took flour, milk and eggs and mixed them altogether.

'A cake must be sweet,' said Puss, so she added sugar.

'And a little bit salty, too,' said Pup, adding salt.

'Next we must put in some butter and jam,' said Puss.

'Not jam,' said Pup. 'I don't like jam. Instead of jam let's put in some cheese. I like cheese a lot.'

So they put in some bits of cheese.

'It looks to me as though it needs to be more fatty,' said Puss. 'We'll have to put in some bacon rind.'

'And nuts, don't forget,' added Pup, emptying some nuts from a paper bag into the mixture.

'Nuts are good,' agreed Puss, 'but there really ought to be some cucumber as well.' And she added a cucumber.

'And bones,' cried Pup, 'we must put in some bones! And a few sausages with plenty of pepper.'

'And now the most important thing of all!' said Puss. 'Whipped cream. We must have some whipped cream.'

So they poured in a whole pot of cream.

'And a little onion,' said Pup, putting one in.

'And chocolate,' added Puss, adding a good large piece.

'And gravy!' Pup remembered, and poured some in.

So they put everything they could think of into their cake and stirred it all up together. When they had mixed all these ingredients together, they stirred them and stirred them. The cake was as large as the wheel of a car!

'Gracious me, this *is* going to be a big cake. Still we'll manage to eat it somehow,' they told each other, thoroughly pleased with themselves. 'And now let's put it in the oven.'

So they put the cake in the oven and waited for it to bake. They were very excited. It steamed and bubbled, spat and sizzled, hissed and spluttered. Then it smoked and frizzled and burnt and boiled over and sent out steam in all directions like a lot of old rags being burnt.

When they thought it was done, they put it on the door-step to cool off.

'You know what,' said Puss to Pup, 'we'll invite the children to share our cake.'

'Yes, rather!' said Pup. 'Let's go and ask them now.'

So off they went, holding paws, to invite the children. They found them in the garden in front of the house, playing marbles. Puss and Pup asked them to come and have some of the cake, but then they played marbles with them for a short while, and after that they played ball, and after that they played bricks a bit.

Meanwhile a nasty spiteful dog came walking by. The cake was cooling off by now and all sorts of delicious smells began to reach his nose.

'Ha, ha, ha!' the spiteful dog thought to himself. 'Something smells good here. It's probably something I like.'

He sniffed and snuffed until he sniffed his way right up to Pup and Puss's cake.

'Ha, ha, ha!' he said, when he got to the cake. 'Here it is. What a feast!'

So he started eating the cake for all he was worth. He gobbled and gobbled until he had tears in his eyes, for the cake was still burning hot inside. He gobbled and gobbled until he had gobbled it all up. Then he washed it down with a canful of water and waddled away.

When Puss and Pup felt they had played long enough with the children, they remembered their cake. So off they all went hand in hand to see if the cake was cool enough to eat.

'It's absolutely scrumptious,' Puss and Pup told the children. 'You've no idea what lovely things we've put ino it!'

When they reached their home and looked around, the cake was gone!

'Good gracious!' said Puss and Pup together. 'Our cake's gone. Somebody's taken it!'

They looked everywhere and, sure enough, they found the spiteful dog lying under a bush groaning horribly. He had eaten much more than was good for him and was now feeling very ill. He had the most terrible tummy-ache.

'Oh my tummy, my tummy!' he wailed. 'Oo, ow, what dreadful things that cake had in it to give me such awful pains!'

'It's your own fault,' said Pup. 'You should have left it alone; it wasn't your cake.'

'To be quite honest, Pup,' said Puss, 'I really don't mind that he ate up our cake. It might have made us ill too, and that would have spoilt our birthday.'

'Hm, true enough,' said Pup. 'Let him groan and moan, horrible spiteful dog. It serves him jolly well right. But I'm hungry. I could eat anything. Only we haven't got anything because we put everything into the cake. It's just not fair. Why should we have to starve on our birthday?'

'Don't you worry, Puss and Pup,' said the children, 'you come along with us and you can have some of our dinner.'

So Puss and Pup went to have dinner with the children. 'Mummy,' said the children, 'here's a dog and a cat; it's their birthday today. We must given them some dinner.'

They had soup and meat and potato dumplings. And mother found them a piece of cake left over from the day before. Puss and Pup enjoyed their dinner very much indeed. They thanked the children for having them and went home very happy.

'What a lovely birthday we've had!' they said to each other. 'Such a gorgeous meal! And not even the tiniest tummy-ache!'

From *Harum Scarum*

Susie Has some New Shoes

JOAN G. ROBINSON

One day Mummy took Susie to buy her a pair of new shoes. Susie took Semolina her doll with her because it was a long time since she had been for an outing and she thought it would be nice for her to see a grown-up shoe shop.

It was a beautiful shop. There was a thick grey carpet on the floor, and in front of each chair was a footstool for people to rest their feet on while they were trying on shoes. And all the way round the walls there were shelves and shelves of white shoe-boxes, reaching from the floor almost to the ceiling.

But the best thing of all was a big rocking-horse with red reins which was standing over in a corner of the shop. Susie sat on a chair beside Mummy and admired it all very much.

'Can I go on the rocking-horse, Mummy?' she asked.

'In a minute,' said Mummy. 'But first we must buy your shoes.'

A lady came to help them choose which kind of shoes they wanted.

She measured Susie's foot with a ruler, then she smiled at Semolina and went off to see if she could find just the right shoes for Susie.

A few chairs away from them another little girl was sitting with her Mummy, and she, too, was having a new pair of shoes bought for her. Susie watched while she tried on first a pair of brown strap shoes, then a pair of blue strap shoes, then some sandals, and last of all some brown lace-up shoes.

The little girl's mummy said, 'Yes, I like those.'

And the little girl said, 'So do I.' And she put the other one on to make sure they were both comfortable.

Just then the lady came back with three pairs of shoes for Susie to try on, but Susie pulled at Mummy's sleeve and said, 'I want real lace-up shoes, Mummy, like that little girl's got.'

Mummy looked, and then she said, 'Well, we might try them.'

So the lady fetched a pair just the same to show them. Susie tried them on and they felt just right, and Mummy said she thought they looked very nice, and so it was all settled. Susie was to have the lace-up shoes.

While the lady was packing them up in a box and Mummy was paying for them Susie ran over to the rocking-horse. A fat little boy was having a ride, and the little girl who had been sitting near Susie was waiting for the next turn. Susie stood beside her.

'Hallo,' said the little girl.

'Hallo,' said Susie.

'I've got some new shoes,' said the little girl. 'They're being wrapped up.'

'So have I,' said Susie. 'Mine are being wrapped up too.'

'Mine are lace-up shoes,' said the little girl.

'So are mine,' said Susie. 'They're just the same as yours.'

'Are they? How funny!' The little girl laughed. 'We'll be just like twins. What's your name?'

'Susie. What's yours?'

'Sara; and my doll's called Briar Rose. What's yours?'

'Mine's called Semolina. I know it's a pudding name really, but I think it's prettier for a girl's name.'

Semolina.

Briar Rose.

'So do I,' said Sara. 'Look, that boy's finished his ride. Will you hold Briar Rose while I have a turn?'

So Susie held Briar Rose while Sara had a ride. Then Sara got down and held Semolina while Susie had a turn. They went on talking while they were having their rides.

'Will you come to my house?' asked Sara.

'Yes,' said Susie. 'And will you come to mine?'

'Yes,' said Sara. 'I've got a doll's house in mine, have you – and a swing?'

'I've got a doll's house,' said Susie, 'but I haven't got a swing yet. I'll come and use yours.'

'Yes,' said Sara. 'Ask your Mummy. Can I have another turn now?'

Sara had just got up again to have a second ride when Susie's mummy called to her to come quickly as she had finished paying and was waiting to go. Susie, who was holding the two dolls, quickly put one of them down and ran off to join Mummy.

'Good-bye!' shouted Sara from the rocking-horse.

'Good-bye!' shouted Susie.

As they went down the road together Susie told Mummy all about Sara.

'She said I could go to her house, Mummy, and I asked her to come to ours.'

'But we don't know where she lives, do we?' asked Mummy.

'Oh, no! What a pity! I forgot to ask,' said Susie. 'And I did want to go on her swing. Oh, Mummy, I *must* go to her house. I promised I would. We were going to have such a nice time.'

Poor Susie was so sad about not knowing where Sara's house was that she couldn't stop thinking about it.

'Couldn't we knock at some doors and ask people if Sara lives there?' she said.

'No, I'm afraid not,' said Mummy. 'You see, we don't even know what road she lives in, and there are too many houses to ask at all of them.'

'She was so nice, Mummy. She said we were like twins because we'd both got the same shoes.'

'Yes,' said Mummy. 'And both your names begin with an S.'

'Oh, yes!' said Susie. 'And we both had dolls. Hers was very pretty. She was called Briar Rose.'

Then Susie gave a little shout of surprise. 'Oh, Mummy, *look*! This is Briar Rose! And I've left Semolina behind with Sara. Oh, what shall we do? Oh, poor Semolina!'

'Well, we'd better go back,' said Mummy. 'Perhaps they will still be there.'

So they hurried back as fast as they could. But when they got to the shoe shop there was no sign of Sara or Semolina.

'I'm afraid they've gone,' said Mummy. 'But we'll ask the lady who sold us the shoes.'

So they waited until the lady wasn't busy and then Mummy explained all about what had happened. The lady was very kind. She knew that Susie must be feeling very sad about Semolina.

'I expect the other little girl will come back,' she said. 'This is a nice doll and I'm sure she won't want to lose her any more than you want to lose yours.'

So in the end Mummy wrote a little note saying she was very sorry about the mistake, and please could Semolina be left at the shop to be called for, and she left Briar Rose and the note with the shop lady who promised to give them to Sara and her mummy if they came back.

The shop lady wrote down Susie's name and where she lived, and then they set off home again, Susie a little bit sad because of Semolina, but still a little bit happy because of the new lace-up shoes.

After tea Mummy let Susie put on her new shoes and practise tying up the bows herself. She was just doing them for the second time when there was a knock at the front door.

Mummy went to open it, and you can guess how pleased

Susie was when she ran out into the hall and found that Sara and her mummy had come. And there, safe and sound in Sara's arms, was dear Semolina!

'How very kind of you to bring her back!' said Mummy. 'I do hope you haven't had to come a long way?'

'Oh, no!' said Sara's mummy. 'We only live in the next road, and we were so glad to get your note at the shoe shop. Sara has been so sad because she forgot to ask your little girl where she lived.'

'And Susie has been so sad because she forgot to ask *your* little girl where she lived!' said Mummy.

'We've only just moved into our house,' said Sara's mummy. 'So we don't know many people here, but Sara would love it if Susie could come and play with her one day.'

'Susie would love it too,' said Mummy. 'And Sara must come here. It will be nice if they can be friends.'

'We are friends already,' said Susie. 'We've even got new shoes the same.'

'Why, so you have!' said Mummy. 'Then Sara must come to tea as soon as she possibly can. Would tomorrow be a good day?'

Sara's mummy thought tomorrow would be a very good day, and so did Sara, and so it was all arranged.

'I am glad we took Semolina shopping with us this afternoon,' said Mummy.

'So am I!' said Sara's mummy.

'And so are we!' cried Sara and Susie together.

From *Susie at Home*

Choosing Shoes

FFRIDA WOLFE

New shoes, new shoes,
Red and pink and blue shoes,
Tell me what would *you* choose
If they'd let us buy?

Buckle shoes, bow shoes
Pretty pointy-toe shoes,
Strappy, cappy low shoes;
Let's have some to try.

Bright shoes, white shoes,
Dandy dance-by-night shoes,
Perhaps-a-little-tight shoes;
Like some? So would I.
BUT
Flat shoes, fat shoes,
Stump-along-like-that shoes,
Wipe-them-on-the-mat shoes
O that's the sort they'll buy.

From *The Very Thing*

The Cat and the Fiddle

PAULINE CLARKE

Once upon a time when cats were cleverer than they are now, there lived in a tidy little cattery a widow cat and her three clever kittens.

Now the eldest kitten was black as coal, and very vain indeed. And the second cat was a cyprus cat, which means she had tabby stripes.

And the third kitten was round like an orange and coloured like an orange, and his name was Tangerine.

Their mamma had not much money, and a very hard job it was to keep going. So she used to grow radishes behind the cattery and sell them for three-pence the bunch to other cats. When she asked the kittens to help tie the bunches they each said something different.

The black kitten said: 'Shan't. I'm greasing my whiskers.'

The tabby kitten said: 'Can't. I'm combing my fur.'

But the youngest tangerine kitten said: 'Very well, Mamma. I'm just coming,' and scampered off to help her.

Inside the cattery were three little baskets belonging to the three kittens; but their poor dear mamma had to sleep on the hearth rug. And on the rug were three little plates belonging to the three kittens, but their poor dear mamma used to eat off the floor.

And the bigger the kittens grew, the more they used to eat, and the less there was left for their poor mamma. In the end they grew so poor, radishes or no radishes, that she did not know what to do. Now it happened that by this time the coal black kitten, who was so very vain, was nearly grown-up.

'Black kitten,' said his mamma to him, 'you must go out into the world and make your fortune. And when you have made it, remember your sister and brother and your poor dear mamma and come back.'

'Very well,' said the black kitten, twirling his long whiskers, 'but what is there in the cattery that I can take with me? I can't go and seek my fortune with nothing.'

So his mamma looked about and she saw in the cupboard his dear papa's black silk top hat. And also his spotted cravat.

'Here,' said she, 'is a black silk hat and a spotted cravat. They will suit you very well.'

The kitten was pleased, and put them on, and cut himself a cane from a raspberry bush. Then off he went down the cattery path, waving at his sister and brother and his poor dear mamma, and determined to seek his fortune.

He walked and he walked until he came to London, and there he met a gentleman walking down the Mall. He had black hair and whiskers and a top hat just like the cat, and carried a cane in his hand.

'There,' said the kitten, 'I should like him for my master: a real rich gentleman in a black silk hat.'

When the gentleman saw the kitten with a hat like his own, he was very pleased and flattered. So they fixed it up between them, the kitten and the gentleman. The kitten wore white spats, and joined the Kit Kat Club, and forgot his dear mamma.

So the days went by, and the kitten never came, so his sister and his brother and his poor mamma stopped hoping, and said: 'He must have found a master.' Which was very true.

Then her mamma said to the second kitten: 'Cyprus kitten, you must go and seek your fortune, and when you have made it, remember your brother and your poor dear mamma.'

'Very well,' said the kitten who was nearly grown-up. 'But may I have something to take with me on my travels? I cannot earn my fortune with nothing at all.'

So her mamma looked all round the cattery, and she found nothing at all but her next-to-best bonnet.

'Here,' she said, 'you may have this bonnet with blue silk ribbons. It will suit you very well.'

The cyprus kitten was delighted, and put on her bonnet, and picked herself a blue flower to wear behind her ear. Then off she went down the cattery path, blowing kisses to her brother and her dear, kind mamma.

When she reached a signpost which said London, she turned round and went another way.

'I don't like London,' said the cyprus kitten. 'I shall go to the country instead to seek my fortune.'

She had not gone very far when she came to a cottage, a sweet, neat, enticing cottage with lavender and catmint growing in the beds, and roses under the windows.

'That's the very place for me,' said the cyprus kitten. 'I wonder who lives there?'

She went up to the door and rattled the handle, tittle-tattle, with her paw. There came to the door a little old woman in a next-to-best bonnet with purple ribbons.

'Well!' she said, shaking her ribbons, 'A sleek, streaky kitten in a bonnet like mine!' And she asked the kitten in. And when they found they liked each other, they arranged to live together. And the cyprus kitten, like her black brother, forgot all about her brother Tangerine and her mamma.

And mamma and the tangerine kitten waited. But the cyprus kitten did not come back, so they very sensibly said to each other: 'I expect she has found a mistress.' Which was exactly true.

'Tangerine kitten,' said his poor dear mamma, 'you will have to go now and seek your fortune, and what I shall do without you I do not know.'

Now the tangerine kitten comforted his mamma, and promised that he would not be long in making his fortune.

'Then,' said he, 'I shall come back and fetch you, and we shall live very happily together ever after. But is there anything I can take to earn my fortune?'

His mamma looked about, and she could not find anything to give to the tangerine kitten for his fortune. But just as they were giving up hope, she found an old fiddle at the back of the cupboard.

'Here,' said she, 'is a very old fiddle. Perhaps you could play it.'

'The older the better,' said the wise little kitten. 'I have always wanted a fiddle.'

So he kissed his mamma, and took his fiddle, and went off down the cattery path to seek his fortune.

Now the first thing he did was to learn to play the fiddle, which was hard for a kitten. But he practised and practised, and as he was a musical kitten, he soon began to learn. He played 'Hey diddle diddle', and 'Hickory, dickory dock', and 'Humpty dumpty', and many other tunes.

He slept in barns and haystacks, and practised in the moonlight.

Now, one fine day, not long after he had left, he came to a village green with a maypole in the middle. All round the maypole pretty girls were gathering, but nobody could dance as there wasn't a fiddler.

'Aha!' thought the tangerine kitten, who was hiding in some trees. 'Here is my chance to make my fortune.' So he went up with his fiddle, and said politely to the people: 'I could play your music, for a very modest fee.'

'A cat and a fiddle!' said the girls. 'Let's try him!'

So the kitten fiddled, and the people danced, until they were all worn out.

'Will you stay with us and be the village fiddler?' said the girls to the kitten.

'Certainly,' said he, 'but I must have a house for two, and I must go and fetch my mamma.'

So he went off again to fetch his mamma. And they both went to live in a cosy cattery made for them near the village green. As the kitten earned his fortune by being a fiddler, his poor dear mamma did not have to grow radishes. She grew catmint and lavender instead.

From *Bel the Giant and Other Stories*

Waggertail and the Thief

JANET WADE

There was once a dog called Waggertail. He was a small lively dog with bright brown eyes. He was a clever dog too and his master, Coco the clown, was sure he could understand everything that was said to him.

Coco and Waggertail were part of a circus and lived in a caravan. Waggertail had learnt to do a few simple tricks with his master. It made the children laugh to see the funny clown and his excited little dog having fun together in the circus ring.

One day Waggertail was running about busily in the circus field, following all kinds of good smells with his nose, when he pricked up his ears. He could hear angry voices coming from behind his master's caravan.

'You had better see that the money is returned by this evening,' said a voice that Waggertail recognized as that of the Ringmaster.

'But I tell you that I didn't steal the money. I don't know where it is at all,' Coco was saying.

'Don't argue with me!' shouted the Ringmaster and off he stalked, his black moustache bristling with anger.

Coco sat down on the steps of his caravan, his pet monkey Jacky on his shoulder. There was a worried frown on his face. He was no longer the happy laughing clown that Waggertail knew.

'Hello, Waggertail,' he said, patting the little dog's head. 'Do you know who stole the money?'

Waggertail shook his tail, which was his way of saying that he didn't.

'Well someone did steal it,' sighed Coco, 'and I wish he'd own up or I'll be losing my job.' Waggertail saw a tear fall on to the clown's big, red shiny nose.

Now the circus people who came at the last minute had to buy their tickets from Coco at the entrance to the big tent that is called the Big Top. When he sold a ticket, Coco put the money into an old tin box and when everybody had gone in, he took the money to the Ringmaster's caravan. 'But last night,' said Coco, 'when I picked up the box it was empty. Whatever can have happened to the money, Waggertail?'

Just at that moment Bilbo, Coco's clown partner, came by.

'Hello, Coco,' he grinned. And then he noticed Coco's unhappy face. 'Hasn't the Ringmaster found the thief yet?'

Coco shook his head sadly. 'He says I must find the money

by this evening and I just don't know where to begin to look. I know he thinks I've stolen it.'

'I wish I could come and help you,' said Bilbo. 'You ought to have someone to keep watch while you sell your tickets. But my act is at the beginning of the show and I have to be ready early.' Bilbo walked away to the ring to practise his act.

'If no one else can help Coco, perhaps I can,' thought Waggertail. He barked and wagged his tail eagerly, tugging at Coco's baggy trousers to attract his attention. Coco laughed and patted the little dog and said, 'Waggertail, you can come with me tonight and watch for the thief. You can be a detective.'

Waggertail didn't know what a detective was, but he meant to find the thief somehow, so he trotted off to a quiet place to think. After all, catching a thief is a very serious business. He knew that many people in the circus were fond of Coco, but everyone was too busy to watch for thieves and the Ringmaster could send Coco away if the money wasn't found.

The time for the circus to begin drew near. Whilst the circus folk were getting ready for their acts and the animals were being groomed for the last time, Waggertail hurried over to the Big Top. He hid himself under one of the tent flaps, only a little way from Coco's table.

'I must be able to see the thief,' he thought, 'but the thief mustn't know I'm watching.' And indeed all that could be seen of Waggertail was two brown eyes and a quivering nose. No one noticed him at all.

The Ringmaster cracked his whip. 'Come along everybody, hurry now. Only a short time to go.'

Along came Coco with Jacky the monkey sitting proudly on his shoulder, dressed in a new red jacket. He was carrying his toy drum by a string round his neck, for Coco had taught him to beat on it to amuse the children in the queue.

Waggertail would have liked to bark a greeting to Coco and to tell him not to worry – he, Waggertail, would catch the thief tonight. But he was quiet in case the thief was around and heard him.

People were arriving already. Family by family they passed Coco and went into the Big Top. Now and then, those who were without tickets, would pay Coco and he would put the money very carefully into the open tin box. Waggertail waited and watched eagerly. For a time nothing happened and then his eyes nearly popped out of his head with surprise. What do you think he saw! While Coco was collecting tickets from the queue and his back was turned, Jacky was reaching down from his shoulder and taking money from the box with his long hairy arm and dropping it inside his toy drum!

Waggertail rushed out of his hiding place and ran to the Ringmaster. 'Come and see,' he barked. 'Come and see what I've found!'

But the Ringmaster was busy. 'Be quiet, Waggertail,' he said crossly. But Waggertail would not be quiet. He tugged at the Ringmaster's coat tails and ran to and fro frantically.

'Whatever is the matter?' the Ringmaster said impatiently. 'I suppose I'd better come and see.'

He followed the excited dog and was just in time to see Jacky scoop up several coins from the tin box and drop them into his drum with a wicked grin, chattering to himself with glee.

'Well, I never!' gasped the Ringmaster. 'Well, I never! So that's the thief.'

Coco had just taken the money from the last person in the queue and was looking into the tin box to see how much he had collected. 'It's gone again!' he wailed. 'Whatever shall I do. I shall be sent away from the circus, I know I shall.'

'Oh no, you won't,' said the Ringmaster and now he was laughing. 'Look in Jacky's drum and see what you can find there.'

Coco seized Jacky's drum and turned it upside down. Out fell a shower of money while the monkey chattered angrily. 'So you were the thief, Jacky!' said Coco accusingly. 'How could you do such a thing?'

'I don't think monkeys understand about stealing,' said the Ringmaster smiling. 'Come now, you must forgive him. He was only playing a naughty joke.'

'Thank you, sir,' said Coco. 'However did you discover the thief?'

'I didn't – Waggertail did. He's our detective,' said the Ringmaster. 'You must thank him.'

If Waggertail could have blushed with pride, he would have done. As it was, he just chased that naughty monkey all round the circus field!

A Christmas Legend

(This is an old story from Brittany. A 'crib' is set up in churches at Christmas time to remind people of the birth of Jesus in a stable. Carved wooden figures of people and animals are grouped round a crib, or bed, as if to worship the baby Jesus.)

There was once a poor farmer who lived in Brittany. His farm was small, just two or three fields in which he grew oats and rye and cabbages and turnips. He had one cow, a few sheep and some pigs. The farmer and his wife and their two children, Pierre and Marie, worked hard. The farmer harvested the crops and milked the cow. His wife looked after the house and the children and made butter and kept hens. The children took the sheep to graze every day.

Each morning early Pierre and Marie drove the sheep to open ground on the edge of the forest. Each morning their mother gave them some bread and cheese to eat during the day, kissed them good-bye and said, 'Be good, little ones!' The children were alone all day but Marie had her spinning and Pierre carved wooden spoons and toys. The sheep were their only companions. It was pleasant to be out in the fresh air in the spring and summer and they enjoyed it then for they were country children. But when autumn brought cold winds and rain and the snow fell in winter, it was a different matter. But most of all they feared the fog for it came creeping across the marshes and blotted out the path home. Even the sheep were uneasy then and crowded round the children as if to seek comfort. There were wolves in the forest and sometimes when they grew hungry they would attack sheep. The children's parents were frightened for them but who else could they send with the sheep?

One winter day – it happened to be Christmas Eve – it was very, very cold. 'Wrap yourselves up warmly, little ones,' said their mother anxiously and she folded Marie's shawl more closely round her and tied Pierre's scarf again. 'It is Christmas Eve, so here are some apples and chestnuts to roast over your wood fire.'

This was a treat indeed, but the children's thoughts were on something else that day. They had seen the Christmas Crib in the village church and it seemed so beautiful to them that they wanted to make one themselves. They had no carved wooden figures to put near the crib – Joseph and Mary, the shepherds and the Wise Men – but, who knows, the Christ Child himself might like to see their crib.

So they settled the sheep to their grazing then began their task. First they lined the hollow in an old oak tree with dry grass and soft green moss. Then they made it beautiful with sprays of dark green ivy and scarlet holly berries and brown pine cones. It was so pretty that they called the sheep to look at it, for after all there were sheep in the fields when the angels sang and the baby Jesus was born. But the sheep were not very interested and soon went back to nibbling the frosty grass.

Then it happened – the fog came drifting across the flat countryside and with it came three grey shapes, wolves! Before the children could do anything to save them, the wolves had caught up three sheep and raced away with them into the forest.

Then Pierre and Marie sat down and cried. They knew how upset their father would be about the sheep and they felt cold and frightened. The fog was all about them and the sheep were uneasy. They lighted a small fire and roasted the chestnuts and apples their mother had given them, but they had little pleasure in the feast ...

There was a faint sound in the fog, as if someone was walking quietly through the dead leaves. Surely no one was coming to this lonely spot? The children stared fearfully into the swirling fog.

And out of the mist came a small boy. His feet and hands were bare and blue with cold and he was crying. Marie did not hesitate for a moment. She ran and took the child in her arms and wrapped him in her shawl and tried to warm his cold feet at the fire. 'Put more wood on the fire, Pierre,' she said busily. Soon the warmth made the child drowsy and it was then that Marie remembered their crib. 'He can sleep in our crib, Pierre,' she said happily. 'What a good thing we have made it so cosy.' The hole in the oak tree was quite large and the child was so small that he curled up in it quite easily, wrapped in Marie's shawl and Pierre's woolly scarf.

For the moment the children had forgotten the wolves and the cold and the fog. Now they remembered their lost sheep. 'How shall we find our way home,' said Pierre, 'and how can we tell father what has happened to the poor sheep?'

'Look, Pierre,' said Marie suddenly. 'A light! It is coming from our crib.'

So it was and it seemed to be all about the child who was waking up now and stretching out his arms to them.

Pierre lifted him down and at once he took their hands and began to lead them through the fog. Trustfully they went with him. And there in the forest was a rough stone barn they had never seen before. Inside were shepherds kneeling on the earth floor. The child let go of their hands and they found themselves alone once more and at their feet were their three lost sheep. The barn and the shepherds were gone but the fog was clearing and a red sun was shining low in the sky.

Joyfully they gathered their little flock of sheep together and hurried home. They told their wonderful story to their mother and she smiled and said, 'Surely that was the Christ Child. He saved both you and the poor sheep, for he loves you both.'

All this happened a long time ago but to this day the people of Brittany believe that sheep are always safe from wolves on Christmas Eve for the sake of the Christ Child.

The Christmas Tree

ANON

Far away in a deep green wood,
A little fir tree shyly stood.
It was so small, so young and weak,
It dare not to its neighbours speak,
For all the trees looked down in scorn
Upon this one so newly born,
When they were all so old and wise,
And such a very goodly size.

But presently there came that way
The Holy Child of Christmas Day,
And when He saw the little tree,
He clapped his hands and laughed with glee.
He danced around it growing there
Among the tall trees proud and fair,
'*You* are my Christmas Tree,' he said
And every tree bowed down its head.

Erminka and the Red-topped Boots

MARGERY CLARK

Once upon a time there was a little girl and her name was
Erminka. When Erminka was exactly four and a half years
old, her Uncle Anton came to her house from the old
country. Erminka's brother was one year and two days
younger than Erminka and much smaller.

Erminka's Uncle Anton brought a set of wooden dolls
for Erminka from the old country. Erminka liked the
wooden dolls, although she did not like most dolls very
much. The dolls' blue dresses were painted on; the dolls'
pink arms were painted on; the dolls' red shoes were
painted on.

Uncle Anton brought Erminka's brother a pair of red-
topped boots. Uncle Anton had bought the red-topped
boots from a shoemaker in the old country. 'I will take a
large pair of red-topped boots,' he said to the shoemaker.
'It is better to have the boots too large rather than too small.
If they do not fit now, they will in a year. Little boys grow
very fast.'

The red-topped boots were too big.

'You will have to wait at least a year before you are large
enough to wear them,' Erminka's mother said.

'Oh, then the red-topped boots will be just right for me!'
cried Erminka, 'for I am just a year and two days older!
May I wear them?'

The red-topped boots were too big for Erminka.

'I can wear three pairs of thick stockings with the red-topped boots, Mother,' she said, 'and then they will fit me.'

In the morning Erminka did not bother to find three pairs of thick winter stockings. She put on her thin white socks and slipped the boots over them quickly.

After breakfast Erminka's mother went into the garden at the back of their house to pick beans and tomatoes. Erminka went along to carry the basket. She wore the red-topped boots.

'I must show my red-topped boots to those tomato plants at the end of the garden,' Erminka said to her mother. 'The red tomatoes and the red tops on my boots are just the same colour.'

She ran down the path in a great hurry.

'See!' she called to the tomato plants. 'My red-topped boots and your red tomatoes are the same colour! Aren't they beautiful?'

Just then Erminka and her red-topped boots slipped. Erminka found herself flat on her back upon her favourite cucumber plant.

'Oh dear! Oh dear! you have crushed a cucumber, Erminka!' cried the tomato plants. 'Oh dear! Oh dear!'

But Erminka had done more than crush one cucumber. She had sat upon ten cucumbers and two juicy red tomatoes and one little bean plant and two fat pumpkins.

In the evening after supper Erminka's mother said to Erminka's father, 'What do you think Erminka did today in the garden?'

'I do not know,' said Erminka's father, as he puffed on his long pipe. 'Had it something to do with the red-topped boots?'

'Yes!' said Erminka and her mother at the same time. 'How did you guess so quickly?'

'I think we shall have to go to the shoe shop and buy Erminka a pair of pretty black slippers,' said Erminka's mother. 'Perhaps then she will not go poking her toes into places where they do not belong.'

'That is a fine idea,' said Erminka's father.

The next afternoon Erminka and her mother set off for the shoeshop to look for a pretty pair of black slippers. On the way they stopped to visit a friend.

The house of Erminka's mother's friend was in a garden full of fruit trees and sweet smelling flowers.

'Let us go and sit in the garden,' said Erminka's mother's friend.

They went into the garden and sat down on a white bench under an apple tree. Soon they began to talk very fast about friends in the old country.

Erminka grew tired of visiting. She ran down to the end of the garden to see the ducks.

Four brown ducks with yellow bills and one large white duck were swimming in a little duck pond at the end of the garden. The ducks swam lazily round and round, until they saw Erminka and her red-topped boots.

'Would you like to see my red-topped boots?' called Erminka.

Two ducks came up to the bank. They pecked at Erminka's boots with their long bills. One big duck came up on the bank beside Erminka.

Erminka was afraid of ducks when they came so close and pecked. Erminka took three steps backwards, away from the duck pond.

The edge of the duck pond was very muddy. Erminka slipped. She sat down with a bump in the soft mud. The little ducks paddled away to the other end of the little pond when they heard the splash. The muddy water splattered on the white feathers of the big duck. He waddled back to the pond. He was very angry.

Erminka's red-topped boots were drenched with mud.

In the evening after supper Erminka's mother said to Erminka's father, 'What do you think Erminka did today?'

'I think I can guess,' said Erminka's father, as he puffed on his long pipe. 'I guess that Erminka bought a pair of pretty black slippers.'

'No, indeed!' said Erminka and her mother at the same time.

Erminka went to the cupboard and brought out the sad-looking red-topped boots.

'I fell in the duck pond,' she said.

'Never mind, Erminka!' said Erminka's father. 'Next week I am going back to the old country for one month. I will go to the shoemaker and buy another pair of red-topped boots that will be just your size.'

From *Poppy Seed Cakes*

Other Puffin collections by Eileen Colwell

TELL ME A STORY
TELL ME ANOTHER STORY
TIME FOR A STORY
BAD BOYS

Some Other Young Puffins

SATURDAY BY SEVEN

Penelope Farmer

Peter should have been saving for a month to get the money needed to go to camp with the Cubs. Now there is only one day left, and how can he possibly earn it in time?

THE WORST WITCH

Jill Murphy

Mildred Hubble had a reputation for being the worst pupil in Miss Cackle's school for witches. So when things started to go wrong at the Hallowe'en celebrations, she was naturally at the centre of it all.

CARROT TOPS

Joan Wyatt

Fifteen stories of everday events like making a jelly, growing a carrot-top garden, visiting Granny – all tinged with the make-believe that young children love.

WHERE MATTHEW LIVES

Teresa Verschoyle

Happy stories about a little boy exploring his new home, a cottage tucked away by the sea.

ADVENTURES OF SAM PIG

Alison Uttley

Ten funny and magical stories about Alison Uttley's best-loved creation. For children of five to nine.

SATCHKIN PATCHKIN

Helen Morgan

Satchkin Patchkin, a little green magic man, lives like a leaf in an apple tree. These stories about him make a book that 'reads aloud so well it is almost a waste to sit alone and read it' – *Times Literary Supplement*

STORIES FOR UNDER-FIVES
STORIES FOR FIVE-YEAR-OLDS
STORIES FOR SIX-YEAR-OLDS
STORIES FOR SEVEN-YEAR-OLDS
STORIES FOR EIGHT-YEAR-OLDS

Sara and Stephen Corrin

Celebrated anthologies of stories especially chosen for each age group and tested in the classroom by the editors.

THE LITTLE SPARROW *and* MIDNIGHT PATROL

Frances Eagar

Two delightful stories about Laura and her brother Harry, in which they befriend a baby sparrow that has fallen out of its nest, and spend a night camping in their wild garden, on jungle patrol.

JOSEPH'S BEAR

Evelyn Davies

The bear was the best thing that Joseph had ever owned, but when you love something you may have to make a hard decision.

THE VILLAGE DINOSAUR
Phyllis Arkle

The cranes had lifted something extraordinary out of the quarry – a real dinosaur, and it seemed to be waking up! Jed Watkins was the first to recognise it, and wanted to keep it in the village as a pet, but the stuffy Parish Clerk wanted to get rid of it before it did any damage.

MY DOG SUNDAY
Leila Berg

Ben longs for a dog of his own, but no one will let him have one. Then one magical Sunday he meets a huge, friendly, shaggy dog in the Park, and nobody seems to own him...

ALBERT'S CIRCUS
Alison Jezard

Albert the bear and his friends think they are off for a quiet holiday in the country – but in no time at all they are hard at work putting on their very own circus show, and what fun it all is!

THE LITTLE GIRL AND THE TINY DOLL
Edward and Aingelda Ardizzone

A tiny doll is dropped into a grocery store's deepfreeze and endures the arctic conditions with the help of a little girl.

Who is he?
He's the mascot of the Junior Puffin Club.

What is it?
It's a reading Club for people who are just beginning to read and enjoy books for themselves.

What do you get?
You have your own badge, membership card and a sheet of stickers when you join and, best of all, you have four copies of a magazine called *The Egg* each year. It's full of stories, competitions, puzzles, bits about authors and artists, and of course, the newest Young Puffins and Picture Puffins.

How do you join?
For further details and an application form send a stamped addressed envelope or label to:

The Junior Puffin Club
Penguin Books Ltd
Bath Road
Harmondsworth
Middlesex UB7 0DA